Scripted
REALITY

KAREN
FRANCES

Jackie

All my love

Karen

x

Dedication

This one is for everyone who has ever doubted themselves.

We all have strength and determination deep within.

We also have weakness and vulnerability and that's not a bad thing.

All these components make us who we are.

Contents

Prologue   1

Chapter One   5

Chapter Two   12

Chapter Three   22

Chapter Four   32

Chapter Five   41

Chapter Six   48

Chapter Seven   54

Chapter Eight   61

Chapter Nine   69

Chapter Ten   77

Chapter Eleven   86

Chapter Twelve   94

Chapter Thirteen   101

Chapter Fourteen   109

Chapter Fifteen   117

Chapter Sixteen   126

Chapter Seventeen   134

Chapter Eighteen   138

Chapter Nineteen   146

Chapter Twenty   153

Chapter Twenty-One   159

Chapter Twenty-Two   *165*

Chapter Twenty-Three   *173*

Chapter Twenty-Four   *179*

Chapter Twenty-Five   *188*

Chapter Twenty-Six   *194*

Chapter Twenty-Seven   *201*

Chapter Twenty-Eight   *208*

Chapter Twenty-Nine   *216*

Chapter Thirty   *222*

Prologue

"I LOVE YOU. SEE YOU in a few weeks." He might be saying the words but I don't see or hear the sincerity in his voice or his actions. The man before me is a stranger. Nothing about him feels familiar. Maybe it's me.

"Love you too," I reply automatically to Donovan as he climbs into the waiting taxi. He's heading back to L.A. for a few meetings. He didn't give me the option to go with him, but that's okay because I want to stay home. I feel as though all I've done this year is travel back and forth. I need some time out. Some time on my own to relax and unwind. But most importantly, to think, without any distractions.

Think about me for a change.

I stand on the front steps and watch as his taxi drives away. He waves, but there's something odd about him today. No, it's not just today. For the past few days he's been on edge, distant, as though there's something bothering him.

He's probably just worried about some contract. That would explain why he's had to rush back to the States. He was meant to be home with me for another few weeks. I'm sure he'll tell me what's wrong as soon as he sorts things out. That's just the way he is; he likes to deal with things on his own.

I turn and head back inside when I see the taxi go through

the gates and then they start to close. I should use this time to catch up with my friends, especially Julie. We've hardly seen each other the past six months with my schedule. But first I plan on tidying up this house, not that it really needs it, but it gives me something to do. Something to occupy my mind.

With music on and turned up loud, I find myself singing along as I work from one room to another cleaning downstairs.

My dad's house keeper does a great job of keeping my house clean and tidy when I'm in the States, but when I'm home I like to do it all myself. I find it therapeutic.

The buzzing of the intercom distracts me as I work in the kitchen. I'm not expecting anyone. "Hello," I say.

"I'm looking for Mr Bell."

"I'm sorry, you've just missed him."

"I have some papers I need to drop off that require a signature." He continues to tell me his name and the company he works for so I can clarify it, which I do, before letting him into the grounds. He's from the company Donovan bought his car from.

I pull the bobble in my hair tighter as I walk through the house. I open the front door to see what looks like a recovery truck. There are two men in it and they both get out. I cross my arms over the front of my body, suddenly feeling intimidated. I wish Donovan was here, or even my dad or brother.

I pull the door closed behind me and walk down the steps.

"What can I do for you?" I ask nervously. One man is wearing a suit, very smart looking and professional, while the other, well, let's just say I wouldn't want to mess with him. He's big, very big, his muscles bulge in his arms and he's scary as he stands looking at me. Reminds me of a good cop, bad cop situation.

"I'm here to recover Mr Bell's car."

"What do you mean?"

"His car is being repossessed. He's not made a payment in

the last six months."

I hear what he's saying but I still don't understand. Repossessed? This must be some sort of a joke, although I'm not seeing the funny side. "Miss, I have all the paperwork here, but I do need the keys."

"Oh," is all I can say as I look at the papers now in my hand. "Does he know?"

"He should. He's been sent letter after letter." I nod, and with the papers still in my hand, I go inside to get the keys. There must be some sort of a mistake. I look at the time but it's too late. I can't call him; his flight has already taken off. I'll give him a call when I know he's landed.

With the keys in my hand, I walk back outside, and the guy I wouldn't want to mess with is already lowering the ramp on his truck. I hand the keys over to the guy in the suit. I sign the paperwork that he sticks in front of my nose, glancing over it briefly. The paperwork confirms that Donovan hasn't paid but this is all weird. It just doesn't make any sense. He hands me over copies that I've to give to Donovan and I stand back and watch as they take away his pride and joy.

I run back inside. None of this adds up. Why would Donovan fall behind with his car payments? I find myself in his office, opening drawer after drawer. I'm not sure what I'm looking for.

Then I find it in the last drawer of his desk. A pile of unopened letters, some addressed to Donovan, but some addressed to me. I start opening them one after another, quickly scanning each. The letters addressed to Donovan all say he owes different companies money; he's behind in not just car payments, but his visa card payments.

With the letters addressed to me in my hand, my body shakes. What are all these? I open the first and try to take in what it says. I sink to the floor and tears fill my eyes. This can't be right.

How is this possible? I've never heard of this company before. What the hell has he done to me? To us?

Chapter 1

WHO'S TO SAY WHAT WAS right for someone five years ago is right for them now? But for some, what was right for them five years ago *is* still right for them.

Everything in life changes on an almost daily basis. People change. Places change. Lifestyles change. Sometimes for worse, sometimes for better.

And why is it we always learn the hard way it's the people you least expect that end up hurting you the most? I suppose that's one of the reasons why it hurts so bad; *because* you don't expect it.

But, then there are always some who will happily stay stuck in the rut they find themselves in. They have no desire to change for anyone. They don't want to push themselves. They drift along in life and it works for them.

Then there are people whose lives change because of circumstances and, more often than not, not for the better. How do they cope when their world comes crumbling down around them?

I've always been told that we adapt to situations that are presented to us. Some people cope with situations better than others. That's a fact.

These are all thoughts that have filtered through my head the past twelve weeks. I've not had much else to do but think when I've been stuck here home alone, while my so-called partner has been across the Atlantic, keeping himself busy with his A-list clients.

Donovan Bell, my unofficial ex. I've learned the hard way recently that, when your boyfriend is an agent to most of the rich and famous in Hollywood, I will always be placed low on his list of priorities.

So, do I just sit back and accept it? No, but under the current circumstances, I'm not sure what I can do.

People talk about the lifestyles of the rich and famous, but I've never really understood why.

Yes, it might look glamorous in the magazines, on TV, and in the newspapers, but in reality, what you see isn't always what you expect.

Take me, for example. Ella McGregor, and before you put two and two together and come up with five, I'm no relation of Ewan McGregor, although I have starred alongside him. I was lucky enough to have a major role beside him in my first big acting job. He looked out for me, saying, 'Us Scots have to stick together.' I liked him a lot; probably my first on set crush.

To the outside world, it appears I have it all; A list of Hollywood blockbuster movies that I've starred in. The looks. The boyfriend. The house. The wealth. Well, the last one is debatable, given my current situation. But what good is all that when I'm having to deal with a whole host of problems on my own as *my* world comes crumbling down?

These problems that have cropped up out of nowhere aren't even mine. I didn't know about half the things in the letters I've received recently, until I read them and re-read them and finally put the pieces of the puzzle together.

Donovan should be here to deal with all this. Explain to me what the hell is happening, but he's too busy wining and dining clients and not answering my calls. He's been in L.A for twelve whole weeks now, but since the day he left me, there has been very little contact. He now refuses to answer my calls. He must have some idea of what the hell is going on here, so I don't get it. I find my anger building towards him with him each passing day.

Angry is good. I can deal with anger. It's better than all the crying I've done lately because I can use that as my motivation to get me through each day. And it's been so damn hard trying to find my strength each day.

If he walked through that front door today, not that I think he will now, the first thing I would do is slap him hard across the face. Who the hell does he think he is? Putting me through all this shit.

What the hell have I done to deserve this?

Over the years, I thought we had a solid relationship that was based on love and trust. But it seems to me, everything I believed has been a lie and I'm left wondering where in the last five years it all went horribly wrong.

It hasn't helped that while I've been trying to deal with all the crap, phoning lawyers and trying to sort out whatever mess he's got us in, he's been seen out and about with various actresses. I've tried telling myself they're only clients, but with his non-communication, it doesn't look good.

There have also been reports in the news speculating about a rift in our relationship. There wasn't before, or maybe there was and I was too blind to see it, but there certainly is now. My mind drifts back to our last few days together. He was so distant and, at the time, I couldn't place what was wrong. Now I know.

So what the hell do I do?

Do I cut my losses with him? Both my personal and professional life, even though he's one of the best agents in the business? Or do I leave things as they are and pretend I know nothing about what's going on?

I'm not some dumb girl who isn't aware of the how bad the situation is. So, no. I can't pretend, especially not to myself. Even though I've found myself pretending to those closest to me that everything is okay.

In my head, for everything he's done to me, he's an ex. I should find myself a new agent but then it would mean admitting I fucked up.

I'm a total mess.

Would I have got some of the parts I've had over the last few years without him? I don't know. I'd like to think my acting would've gotten me the parts without him, but I'm sure he played a major role.

Have I come to any big decisions? No. Although I know what I should do.

My life is too fucked up at the moment. But I should speak to him. If he would only communicate with me, maybe then I'll be able to make the right decisions for me and my future.

My future alone. Without him.

Up until this all started, Donovan was the love of my life. He was the one I saw my future with. But now, I feel as though my whole life hangs in the balance. I'm at a crossroads and I don't know which way to turn. I feel as though I'm standing in front of a sign, directions mapped out before me, but they're blurry so I don't know what to do. What if I take the wrong path and it leads me to a dead end?

What then?

Will I be able to find my way back to the correct path?

I see my future at home in Scotland, not in L.A. and not with Donovan who would much rather be there. L. A. is his home, after all. He's never really settled here in Scotland.

He's taken so much from me. Destroyed me from the inside out. I hardly recognise myself anymore.

The last few years, my time has been split equally between here and the States, because of my workload. But for now, I don't want to split my time. I'd love nothing more than to settle down, maybe even have a family at some point in the future. But as for my career, I have no idea what I want. I just know that I don't miss the constant party scene that comes with living in L.A.

When I was young, I always dreamt of being rich and famous. I just wanted to be like my dad, the man who could never do any wrong in my eyes, and still can't. I always wanted to act or sing. My singing voice is okay, but I learned at a young age it would never really make me any money.

I suppose it's easy for me to say money isn't my driving force, but I really do love acting. In the beginning, I, like many others actors, was probably totally taken in by the amount of money I was making and, of course, all the recognition that comes with being famous.

The recognition drives my friends daft when we're out for a night in town and we get stopped and I'm asked for pictures, autographs etc. I used to love it. I'm not sure what's changed in me, but it's obvious something has.

Is it because I'm about to lose everything I've worked damn hard for over the years? That's a very big possibility.

Donovan Bell has a lot to answer for. The first sign of any trouble was the day he left when his car was repossessed. Panic gripped me tightly that day, as I realised the extent of my problems. Problems that wouldn't disappear and certainly couldn't be ignored. Although, for a few weeks, I did ignore them until I realised that would only make matters worse.

I cried a lot and shut myself away from family and friends. Once my tears gave way, I did the only thing I could and phoned my lawyer, Jonathon, to see if he could find out what the hell was going on. Seems like my so-called boyfriend had got himself into a spot of bother, and he seems to be pulling me under with him.

Jonathon wanted me to let my dad know straight away, but I refused to tell him and so I avoided him as best as I could.

It didn't take long for Jonathon to get back to me; this house that I own I bought outright after my very first movie; no mortgage, no finance. Nothing. Well, Donovan has somehow managed to re-mortgage it *and* re-finance my two cars. I face the possibility of them being repossessed. There's no money in our joint bank account and barely anything left in my own personal account. My bank manager is looking into that because, as Donovan has emptied my account, fraud has been committed.

I want to wrap my hands around Donovan's neck and squeeze life from him slowly, because these last few weeks he's drained life from me. I'm not sleeping. I've lost weight. I've hardly left the house, and that isn't me. When I'm here at home in Scotland, I always make time for my friends and family. I know they're getting worried, but I don't know what I would say to any of them. I'm embarrassed about what's happening, even though I have no control over it.

It's funny, with everything that's happened, it's made me realise I've lost myself somewhere over the last five years. I've lost the strength of the independent woman I was and I've become the one thing I swore to myself I would never be. I've become dependent on a man.

And not just any man. A man who I loved and trusted wholeheartedly. But Donovan has lied to me, stolen from me and, from the news stories coming from Hollywood, he's probably cheating on me too. But I've not wanted to hear the stories. I switched the TV over.

Reality has brought me back down to earth with a bump.

I turn and face my bedroom mirror; my light brown hair is lifeless, my eyes look as though they have sunken into my face, and the black circles underneath are proof of my sleepless nights. I just wish this mess was sorted out.

For someone with so many connections in the world, how the hell has he managed to get himself and me into such a bloody mess?

My body shakes as I feel the strain of the past few weeks

getting to me. Lack of food and sleep are bound to have an effect on me. Tears fall from my eyes and, in this moment, I'm not sure if there's a way out for me, because I'm not about to ask anyone other than my lawyer for help. I just hope he finds a way out before I lose everything I've worked hard for. It might be nice if he could get the answers to the thousands of questions spinning around in my head. The biggest one being; why has Donovan done this to me? To us? The woman he was meant to love. I thought he would be my forever.

Clearly, I was wrong.

Chapter 2

MY PHONE BEEPS. I'M SURE this is another text from my friend Julie, checking up on me, wanting to meet up. The first few weeks after Donovan left, I kept saying I was busy with work, and then she was away on holiday for a month. Recently, I've declined all her offers of catching up, making up excuse after excuse. I'm running out of excuses now and I'm sure she knows it. I pick up my phone but it's not Julie.

A sudden coldness creeps over me, sending shivers down my spine as his name flashes before me. It's Donovan:

Flight no BA3212 arriving Glasgow International @3.20pm today.

I stare at my phone. What the . . . ? So, just like that, he expects me to drop everything and go running and pick him up from the airport? Of course he does, and I'll go because we have things to discuss. No contact for all this time and, suddenly, this. Something is going on. I just need to find out what. I should call Jonathon and let him know Donovan will be back in the country today.

For the last twelve weeks, all Jonathon has wanted to do is drag his sorry arse back to the UK to face up to what he's done. He was even prepared to fly out and get him himself.

I hope I find the strength to deal with Donovan today.

Today's not a bad day. So far, no panic attacks, no tears, and

I've managed to get myself out of bed, so I'm off to a good start. With another glance in the mirror, I'll do. What's the point in even trying to make myself look better? He needs to see what he's done to me. See how I've dealt with the stress he's caused. My face is thin and pale. I need some sunshine. That thought is funny, because L.A. has lovely sunshine and warm temperatures. I'm sure he'll look all healthy with a tan while I just look ill.

I look around the room and, even though all my belongings are here, it doesn't feel like me. With a shake of my head, I leave the comfort of my newly appointed bedroom and slowly make my way along the hallway and down the stairs. As I reach the bottom stair, there's a loud knock at the front door. The only people who have the code to the main gates are my dad, my brother, and Julie. I freeze, remembering. They're back. How could I forget they would be home today from their holiday?

Dad and Callum.

Oh, no. My heart is racing in my chest and there's a heavy feeling in the pit of my stomach. I cover my mouth and try taking a deep breath, because I think I'm about to be sick.

I look down at my clothes, which are hanging from me because I've lost so much weight. I don't need to stand on the scales to see the numbers; it's completely visible for all to see. I suppose that's one of the reasons I've been putting Julie off as well.

Dad and Callum will know something is wrong as soon as they see me. What can I tell them? Do I lie or tell them the truth?

The front door opens and a cool breeze fills the hallway. Callum has used his key. He does always knock before coming in, so I know it's him. They both enter, tanned and refreshed from their golfing holiday. They've been in the South of France for the last three weeks, mixing business with pleasure. Dad's smile instantly changes as he takes in my appearance. I drop my head in shame and I know without a shadow of a doubt that my tears aren't far away.

I've hidden this for so long, but I know, I just know deep down I can't hide it any longer. They're going to be angry with me.

"Bloody hell, sis. Are you ill?" Callum is by my side, taking my arm in his and ushering me into my front sitting room. I can hear my dad's footsteps following closely behind us and I've been dreading this moment because I know I won't be able to keep this from either of them. I'm glad Callum is holding me because, truthfully, I don't think I'd still be on my feet if it wasn't for him. The room is spinning and my head hurts.

He sits me down on the sofa and sits beside me, wrapping his warm, strong arms around my cold body. "Ella, please. You have to tell us what's wrong."

"Sweetheart." Dad's voice is gentle. I lift my head, and when I see the look of concern and sadness in his eyes, I crumble and my tears fall. He bends before me and Callum releases his hold as I fall into my dad's strong arms. "Ella, you have to tell us what's wrong. I'm imagining all sorts of things and none of them are pretty."

With a sniffle and a deep breath, I wipe my eyes. "No, I'm not ill. Although that might be better than what I have to tell you."

My dad and brother exchange concerned glances. "Ella . . . whatever it is can't be that bad."

"Donovan has fucked up."

"There's a surprise," Callum says, and I can hear his sarcasm. He's never been Donovan's biggest fan. I've never really understood why, to be honest, until recently. Callum obviously saw something in Donovan that I couldn't. I'm sure this will be the moment he says, 'I told you so.'

"I don't know how he's managed it, really I don't, but Jonathon and my bank manager are looking into everything for me."

"What has he done?" Dad's tone changes from sweet and caring to demanding.

Tears roll slowly down my face. You would think I wouldn't have many of these damn things left to fall, but the tears keep coming. "He's re-mortgaged my house and cars and withdrawn everything from my bank accounts."

"You mean you have nothing left?" Callum asks the question. I turn to him, close my eyes and nod.

"Sweetheart." I open my tear-filled eyes and turn back to my dad. "When did you find this out?"

"A little over twelve weeks ago when his car was repossessed," I mutter. I know he's going to be mad. I've managed to avoid this conversation with them because I used every excuse in the book not to go to events with them before they went on holiday.

Dad's nostrils flare and his face reddens. "Fucking hell, Ella. Why didn't you come to me straight away? Three bloody months!"

"I don't know. Embarrassment. Maybe."

"Ella, Ella. What am I going to do with you? What's Jonathon saying? What about Donovan? What's he got to say for himself?"

I'm in two minds about telling Dad about Donovan's text message, because if I know my dad as well as I think I do, he'll be at the airport to meet him. And it won't be a pleasant meeting. I have a vision in my head of my dad pinning Donovan up against a wall before he thumps him one, and I wouldn't blame him. "I've tried to call him several times, but he's not answering."

"Ella, sweetheart, you'll have to give me all the information you have. I'll deal with this for you now because I don't want my daughter ill. Callum, go and make your sister something to eat. Even a bit of toast."

I bow my head in shame. "I've not been shopping."

"Are you telling me you've no food in this house?"

"Yes."

"No wonder you look ill. This is ridiculous. Wait until I get my hands on Donovan. I'll bloody kill him, or I'll make this common knowledge and he'll never work a day again. For anyone." Dad's voice is venomous. "I'm taking you out for something to eat. Callum is going to go shopping for you. Then I'm treating you to a hair cut or some other pampering session while I go and meet with Jonathon and see what I have to do to make this mess go away. Not for Donovan, for you. Then I'll deal with him at a later date. Do I make myself clear?"

I look at Callum. He's got a sad smile on his face but he nods in agreement with our dad. I'm not sure I'm in the right state of mind to be going out, but when my dad makes up his mind on something, there's no arguing with him. "Thank you," I say, turning back to face him.

"You never need to thank me. I'm protecting my own and your mother would be turning in her grave at what's going on. She would be so upset if she could see you now. Jesus, Ella. I thought I was going to lose you. I really thought you were seriously ill. This is fixable. We'll get you through this. But I am mad with myself for not picking up on the signs that something was wrong in the weeks before we went on holiday. And then the constant rumours in the gossip columns the last few weeks about you and him. I'm not much of a father, am I? I should have been here for you." I throw my arms around him, resting my chin on his shoulder and allow my tears to fall. I feel Callum's hands on my back, rubbing it gently, trying to comfort me.

"I'm so sorry. This isn't your fault."

I've been so stupid in keeping this to myself.

After a few minutes, my tears stop.

"Right, let's go and get you fed," Dad says, standing and holding his hand out to me. "Maybe even get you some clothes that fit you."

"I love you," I say, taking his hand.

"I know you do and I love you, you crazy, crazy girl. Don't you ever forget it."

THIS IS JUST what I needed; time away from the house. Away

from all my problems. Callum has gone back to my house with shopping and Dad has gone to Jonathon's office. No doubt he'll give him a piece of his mind for not telling him what's been going on. We spoke at great length when we went for something to eat. I told him I didn't want to lose my house if it could be avoided. The other stuff, cars, I'm not too bothered about. But my house holds lots of special memories for me.

My mum came with me to view it and we both fell in love with it the minute we stepped inside. It was also an added bonus that it was only a ten-minute drive away from her and my dad. We've all spent many a Christmas around my dining table, laughing and joking before moving to my front room to relax with a glass of wine, watching the flames dance in the log fire.

Yes, I know at the end of the day it's only a house, but it's one I see me staying in all my life. I had the house before Donovan and I got together and hopefully, with my dad's help, I'll still have it after we go our separate ways because I know that's what has to be done.

I sit in front of the mirror and my usual hairdresser is huffing and puffing about the condition of my hair, and I really don't blame her. It's been twelve weeks since I was last here but the stress of these last few weeks has certainly played havoc with my hair. It's a mess, much like the rest of me.

"Okay, I can do something with this, but you need to get back to regular appointments. I can tell you're stressed about something, but it's not my place to question you. I'm sure you get enough of that when you walk down the street." I smile at her reflection. "Now, it's my job to not only make you look better, but feel better. Then, once we have your hair done, I'll get one of the other girls to do your nails."

When I sat down, she asked what I wanted done with my hair. I told her, "Do what you like." She seemed surprised but told me she wouldn't do anything too drastic. She chats away as she puts the colour on my hair. The thing about coming here is, I always feel normal. Strange, I know, but all the staff just see me as a regular client. They don't fuss around me and, when you live your life in the public eye, feeling normal is good.

I'm at the furthest work station from the entrance, but I have a clear view of the salon and the front door. The door opens and in comes a girl, I think in her late teens. She scans the salon as she speaks to the lady at the reception desk. She looks in my direction and I look away, not wanting her to recognise me, but I think it's too late. I catch the excitement on her face in the mirror before me.

The stylist hands me a few magazines and a cup of tea when she finishes putting the colour on. I enjoy this time when I get to sit and relax with my own thoughts. Today, though, I'm trying hard not to think about the small fact that, in only a few hours, I'll be seeing Donovan.

Instead of sitting in the hairdressers, I should be at home packing his belongings so he can leave my house. I don't want him there. I don't want him in my life now. Not in any capacity. Everything seems so much clearer now after talking to my dad and Callum, even though my brother was just agreeing with everything Dad said.

My dad, the great Scottish actor Archie McGregor, but to me, he's just my dad. The only man in the world I've truly looked up too. My mum always said I would follow in my father's footsteps, and she was right. I'm so glad she got to see some of my accomplishments before she was so cruelly taken from us. She died three years ago after a really long and brave battle with cancer. Right up to the very end, she was still fundraising and raising awareness of the disease that now affects one-in-five people.

Sheena McGregor was an inspirational woman. A wife, a mother, and then her career and all her charity work. She was a TV presenter and, as much as she loved her job, her family was and remained the most important part of her life right up to the end.

"You're her. You really are Ella McGregor" The young girl that entered the salon a few minutes ago is standing at my side, staring at me. She digs into her pocket. "Can I get a picture with you?" My stylist quickly comes to my rescue as the girl takes her phone from her pocket.

"No you don't," my stylist says, pulling her phone from her hand. "All my clients deserve privacy in the salon and Miss Mc-Gregor is no different."

"I'm s . . . sorry," she stutters. "I didn't mean any harm. It's just I love you and love everything you've starred in."

"Thank you. No harm done," I say softly. The stylist ushers her away, telling her she'll return her phone when she's leaving the salon. That seems a bit harsh, but then again, I don't want to open tomorrow's papers and see me on one of the pages with these foil papers on my head and no make-up on.

I flick through the magazines, not reading or paying attention to any of the articles until one catches my eye. Donovan with a very relaxed and refreshed Katherine Hunter; the American actress who has spent a lot of time undergoing counselling. She's been out of the spotlight now for well over a year. No new movies, nothing. In the picture, they look very cosy in some restaurant. I try to dismiss the picture the same way I've dismissed all the others I've seen in recent weeks, but there is something different about this one.

It's the sparkle in her eyes as she looks at him. Something about how close they appear to be. Everything about this picture tells me they're a couple. My eyes drift to the article that accompanies the picture. There's nothing factual in the article. It appears to be someone giving their opinions on the pair and it doesn't tell me who has written it.

Rumours about Katherine Hunter's health have been in full swing lately. She's an actress who has lived her life in the public eye for so long.

I'm sure she's hoping her latest stint in hospital undergoing counselling will be her last.

Over the years, her life has been very publicly documented, ever since she wrongly accused Mr Alexander Mathews of a crime he didn't commit. That incident resulted in her finally seeking help for a traumatic event that happened in her childhood.

Now, though, she is not only looking better, according to our sources, her career might be about to take off again with the help and support of Donovan Bell. But the question on everyone's lips is; how close are Mr Bell and Miss Hunter? And where does that leave the very beautiful and bonny Ella McGregor?

I'm sure we will all find out in due course.

Bloody hell. I stare at the page before me. While I'm here trying to sort out a mess he has caused, he's getting up close and personal with Katherine Hunter. Yes, it hurts seeing him with 'clients', but now I know better. When I start to feel upset, I think about all the pain he's caused me.

Why is he coming here today? After all this time. What is it he wants? I'm hoping I can put some sort of closure between us and have him out of my life once and for all once my dad and Johnathon sort things out. There's been talk about criminal proceedings against Donovan because what he's done is illegal.

But in all fairness, I don't know what I want to do about that. For one, it would cost me to start the ball rolling, and I know my dad would be more than happy to help me out financially, but I don't want to rely on him. I need to get back on my feet. Be able to support myself again.

"Okay, Ella. Let's get this colour washed off and then I can give you a new look," the stylist says.

IT'S AMAZING WHAT getting your hair done can do. A good hairdresser is worth her weight in gold when she can turn how you feel around, and mine has certainly done that. My light brown hair no longer looks or feels lifeless because of all the blonde highlights through it, and a good two inches at least has been cut off. So, courtesy of my dad, I've had my hair and my nails done and even bought a few new clothes that fit me instead of hanging on me like a sack of spuds.

Now I stand dressed in jeans, a nice top, and a pair of black heels, feeling almost human, at the arrivals of Glasgow International Airport. I'm slightly uneasy at the thought of seeing Donovan walk through those doors. I've already checked and double checked and his flight landed about thirty minutes ago, so any minute now, he'll be here.

As I drove here, I tried to think of what I would say to him, but nothing came to me. I have questions that need to be asked, but I'm not sure I'm ready for the answers. I already know he'll try and fob me off and I'm sure the first thing he'll say to me is, 'I've missed you and I love you.'

Those are not the words he'll hear from me.

People start coming through the doors and I move from one foot to the other as I wait. My heart is racing. I run my fingers through my hair.

"Shit!"

Where the hell is Donovan? I'm confused. He is not who I expected to see.

He smiles at me briefly and then looks over his shoulder to see what I'm staring at. When no one else comes through the doors, he turns back to me and shrugs his shoulders.

Donovan Bell is nowhere to be seen and I swear to God, all I want to do now is kill that bloody man.

Instead, I'm standing face-to-face with one of Donovan's best friends.

Chapter 3

CONNOR ANDREWS.

The last person I thought I would be seeing today. I take a deep breath, partially relieved that I don't have to deal with Donovan after all. I was so unsure how I would react to seeing him. Part of me thinks he would've said something sweet and I would've melted into his arms, forgetting about everything he's put me through. The other part thinks I might've caused a scene here in the airport as I mouthed off at him, telling him exactly what I think of what he's done.

My eyes scan Connor's body, taking him in. It's been a few months since I last saw him, but he still looks as perfect as ever. From the way his dark hair sits to the way his jeans hang low on his hips. My eyes pause for a brief moment on the hem of his white t-shirt because I happen to know that what is underneath it is as perfect as the rest of the man before me. From looking at him, you'd think he hadn't just spent hours sitting on a plane.

I stand for a moment, taking in his tempting, attractive male physique that has women falling over themselves for his attention.

And today it would seem I'm one of those women.

Why? I don't know. As if I don't have enough things on my mind to be confused about, my emotions are now playing with my head.

Connor Andrews is a confident man. He's a friend, but today, since the first time I met him, I'm suddenly very wary of the man before me.

"What the hell are you doing here?" I snap, pulling my eyes back to his face. I watch as his smile turns to a puzzled look.

He puts his bag down and removes his hand from his case then leans forward, wraps his arms around me, and kisses me on the cheek. "Eh, good to see you too *my* gorgeous Ella." He draws his head back, leaving his arms where they are and looks me over. If I didn't know any better, I'd say he was checking me out. Actually, I know he is; this is what he does. His brown eyes never leave my face, and wrinkles form around his eyes as he frowns at me. "Your hair looks amazing. I love the colour, it really suits you, but the rest of you, not so much. You've lost too much weight. You can tell me what's wrong when we're back at the house."

Of course Connor would notice there's something wrong with me. "You're staying with me?" He nods. Brilliant. Why I'm surprised, I don't know, because he always stays at my house when he's back on home soil. I have a lot of time for Connor; he's been a good friend to me over the years, but he's also one of Donovan's closest friends.

Donovan should've at least told me Connor was arriving and staying with me. Why couldn't he just stay at a hotel? Or better still, finally buy himself a house here. He spends more than half the year here in Scotland, usually staying with Donovan and me. Occasionally, he spends a few days with his parents up north. "Sorry, but I didn't expect you."

"So, what are you doing here then?"

"I thought I was collecting Donovan," I say, my voice lower than it was moments ago.

"Well, I'm sorry to be such a huge disappointment," he says, chuckling. I have to stop myself from telling Connor I'm more relieved it's him. He releases his hold of me, picks up his bag, and grabs his case handle. We leave the airport side-by-side in silence. What the hell am I meant to tell him about what's been going on here? I don't want Donovan to find out that I know what he's done. Not yet. And does Connor know what his friend has been up to lately?

"So, how long are you staying?" I ask. Maybe it will give me an inkling as to when Donovan will be back in the country, but then again, this is Donovan. I think there's more chance of me being in L.A. before he comes back to Scotland, and at the moment, I'm not ready to be in L.A. If I'm honest with myself, I'm not sure I'm ready to see Donovan.

"Well, the premiere of my new film *code breaker* is next week, and I don't have any plans. So, I'm not sure. How long will you be able to put up with me?" He smirks.

"A day," I say with a straight face. And even that might be too long.

He flutters his eyelashes and then winks at me. "I'm sure I can persuade you to let me stay longer." This is typical Connor. He thinks a bit of harmless flirting can get him anything he wants.

"We'll see. I have a lot going on." Instantly, I regret the words that have slipped from my tongue. I can see him from the corner of my eye, watching me as we walk toward the car. I know I shouldn't have said anything because I'm bound to have raised his suspicions and his loyalties are to Donovan, not me. They were friends long before Donovan and I got together.

We stop at my car and I open the boot. Connor puts his case and bag in then closes it. I stand at the side, and he turns and walks toward me, taking my hand in his. "Ella, I'm your friend. Whatever is going on, you can tell me. If I can help, I will. I want to."

His words set off a reaction, one that, whilst he's here, I'd rather keep to myself. My lips start to tremble and I desperately will them to stop, but tears are already forming in my eyes. I turn my head away from him, fighting back my tears, not wanting him to see that I'm upset.

"It's too late, Ella. I can see you're upset. Please tell me." His hand touches my face and gently turns it back so I'm facing him. I flinch at his touch, a slight chill running through my veins. He removes his hand from my face, running it through his hair and, for the first time since I've known him, he looks so confused. "Ella, I would never hurt you. Please. There's something wrong. You've never looked as scared as you do right now. Who hurt you?"

"I don't want to talk about it." I turn my face to the side, staring at nothing for a moment. People and cars can be heard and seen moving around in the background, but I'm not paying attention to those. I'm trying to compose myself because I can feel panic setting in and now isn't the time for a panic attack. My breathing is accelerated and I take a few long, deep breaths in an attempt to slow it down. It works. It should. Over the last few weeks and months, I've had plenty of practice.

"What you really mean is you don't want to talk to me about it. So, I guess this is about Donovan," he says sadly, breaking the trance I'm in.

"It doesn't matter," I say, shrugging away from him. I hear a long sigh but I don't turn back. Instead, I get into the driver's seat and wait for him to get in the car. Already, I know it's going to be hard for me to be around him.

I ENTER THE code for the gate and tap my fingers against the steering wheel, waiting not so patiently for it to open. Today of all days, everything seems to be going in slow motion, when all I want is for this day to be over so I can be tucked up in bed. The metal gates finally open enough for my car to drive through. It's then I see my dad's car along with Callum's parked to the side of the driveway.

This isn't what I need today.

I stop the car and my front door swings open. Callum almost bounces down the stairs. I climb out. "We were starting to get worried about you. Where have you been?"

"I had something to . . ." I don't get to finish what I'm saying. Callum's eyes shift to the passenger side of my car.

"Yeah, I can fucking see that. What the hell is he doing here? And where is his friend? That useless waste of space? I swear if he's in the country I'll fucking kill him for what he's put you through."

"Hold on a minute," Connor says, walking around the car. I could leave them all to it if I wanted to. I'd run inside and straight up the stairs and hide away in my bedroom and not listen to the argument I'm sure is about to happen. But as I look toward the door, my dad is standing there, casting his eyes over the situation in my driveway. There's nowhere for me to hide now.

"It's just as well your sister has no neighbours." My dad's voice echoes loudly around us. I try to smile but I'm finding it hard. "Let's get inside, please, and then you can tell us what's going on."

I nod and look at Connor who looks totally bewildered. He walks to the back of my car and opens the boot to get his belongings. "Callum, help Connor." It's not a question from my dad, but a statement. Callum huffs and mumbles under his breath but he does go and help. "Sweetheart, I've put the kettle on and taken care of all outstanding bills that I found in the office. We can talk about that later, and if there's anything else that needs attention, I'll sort that too."

"Thanks," I say, wishing he didn't have to, but grateful that he has. One less thing for me to worry about.

"By the way, the new hairstyle. I love it." Dad kisses me on the head and wraps his arm around my waist and we walk through the house together to the kitchen. Dad always noticed when Mum had been to the hairdressers. I remember him paying her compliments about her hair and, toward the end, about her wigs. Some men don't notice these things, but Dad always did.

I sit down at the island as my dad makes four cups of tea and we wait for Callum and Connor to join us. I can hear them talking out in the hallway but I don't hear what's being said.

It was strange hearing Callum shouting at Connor, because the two of them have also become good friends over the years, despite the fact my brother doesn't like Donovan. I hope all this crap with Donovan doesn't change that, but I have a feeling it will. It's bound to.

The guys come into the kitchen just as Dad places the cups down on the island before me. "Okay, Ella. You have some explaining to do."

"Yes, I know. Dad, I'm sorry. Donovan texted me this morning with flight details. Maybe I should've told you, but I wanted to see him first on my own. I thought . . . oh I don't know what I was thinking. His message just said a flight number and time and I presumed I would be picking him up from the airport, but when I got there it was only Connor. Sorry." My last word is meant for Connor, and he offers me a small smile. Poor guy. He has absolutely no idea of what the hell is going on.

"Connor, where is Donovan?" my dad asks.

"He's still in L.A. I'm not sure what's been going on but I thought he'd told Ella I was coming, but it was very clear to me at the airport she didn't have a clue. What's going on? I get he's done something that has upset you." Connor looks directly into my eyes and, although I want to look away from him, I can't. Something is holding me hostage, just like earlier in the airport.

"He might be in on it," Callum snaps. "Playing games with Donovan. Hurting my sister."

"Bloody hell, Callum. If he's hurt Ella do you really think I would be in on it? Come on, you of all people should know me better than that. I have no idea what's going on. Why don't you just tell me?" A look I can't quite place passes between my brother and Connor, and Callum nods as though he understands. I'm glad someone does, because I don't.

Dad looks at me and I nod. "It seems your friend has got himself into a spot of financial trouble and he's trying to pull my daughter down with him."

"I don't understand. What do you mean?"

With a deep breath, I say, "What Dad means is that somehow Donovan Bell has re-mortgaged *my* house and re-financed *my* cars along with emptying all my bank accounts. I only found out this information after his car was repossessed."

Connor places his cup down slowly and sits back in the chair, thinking about what I've just said. "Are you sure? Of course you are; a new hairstyle isn't going to hide the small fact that you look as though you haven't slept or eaten properly in weeks. But how? He's still been out on the town night after night splashing the cash."

"Yes, I know he has, while I've been stuck here without a penny. No money for food or to pay the bills." My dad closes his eyes; obviously this is hard for him to hear. But I'm not going to hide the truth from any of them, not anymore. The last few weeks have been really tough, trying to deal with everything on my own.

"Honestly?" Connor asks.

"Yes," I reply, completely deflated.

"But how?" he asks my dad.

"I have no idea. This was all news to me and Callum this morning."

Connor reaches across the table and takes my hand in his. "Ella, you, crazy, stupid girl. Why the hell didn't you tell anyone? You have good friends and family who love you and we would do anything for you. I just don't understand." His voice is laced with sadness and his eyes are filled with . . . I actually don't know what his eyes are filled with.

"Lots of reasons. Embarrassment being the biggest. I feel like such a fool."

"You have nothing to be embarrassed about. I want to fucking kill him myself. What is he playing at? Is there anything I can do to help?" Connor asks my dad but keeps his hands in mine.

"At the moment, no. Our lawyer is looking into everything. At least Ella had the common sense to involve him from the start. It looks as though if Ella wants to keep the house, I'll have to pay off the mortgage company and the same with the cars. Then I'm not sure if we'll get anything back if we take him to court because he's taken credit out with various companies and there's nothing in any of his bank accounts. Both private and business. As I said, the lawyer is looking into it to see exactly where Ella stands."

"Ella, I'm so sorry. I really had no idea."

"This isn't your fault. But haven't you noticed anything different about him?" I ask.

"I've not been in his company much the last few months. You know how it is. As soon as I was finished filming one movie, I was straight onto another set. I've not had a minute to myself. This is the first and all I wanted to do was be here in Scotland with y . . . amongst friends." I might have a lot going on, but I did catch his slip of the tongue. I try not to think about what he was going to say. "He did say he had a few things to do in L.A. but would be here for my film premiere."

"If he thinks for one minute he's coming here, he had better think again," Callum shouts, banging his cup on the counter. Not much gets my brother angry, except someone hurting me. He's always been the same, even when we were kids. He always wanted to look out for and protect me, even though I'm two years older than him.

"He won't be staying here," I say, but as the words leave me I don't really know what I'll do about Donovan. "Can we not talk about it? This whole situation is leaving me drained. Connor, what's next for you?" I ask, changing the subject. Three sets of eyes stare at me.

"I'm not sure. I wanted to talk to you about that, see what you thought of the proposal for the Glasgow based soap opera."

"What proposal?" I ask, looking at him then glancing back to my dad.

"You mean Donovan hasn't sent you the proposal? This is getting stranger by the fucking minute."

"You're telling me."

"I can pull my copy up from my emails and let you see it. On it you will clearly see they want both of us and are more than happy to work around our other commitments."

"Sweetheart, I think it's safe to say you're going to need a new agent."

"I know, but the minute word on that gets out there's going to be lots of speculation about me and Donovan."

Dad squares his shoulders. "There already is lots of speculation. You've been too busy hiding yourself away, dealing with his crap to really take notice. Ella, I can make all the money issues go away, you know that . . ."

"I do, but you shouldn't have to bail me out," I interrupt. I should ask about the speculation, find out for myself what is being said, but at the moment I'm just not interested.

"Enough," Dad snaps. "You're my daughter and I, like all other fathers in the world, won't sit back and watch as that man destroys everything you've worked so hard for. Now, you have to leave lawyers and Donovan to me. It's time for you to concentrate on yourself. Get yourself looking and feeling one hundred percent." Callum and Connor nod in agreement. I'm outnumbered.

"And you should start with eating a proper meal," Callum tells me. His eyes are full of sadness. "The fridge and cupboards are now full, so no excuses. *Please?*"

"I promise. Dad, do what you have to do," I say reluctantly. "Do you both want to stay for dinner?"

"We can't. I have a few things to take care of and your brother has a date."

"A date? Who?"

"It's not a big deal. Just someone I know," he says without looking at any of us. His body language tells me this is a big deal, so I'm not going to push the subject. I know if anything comes of it, he'll tell me.

"So, it's just you, me, and a proposal tonight," says Connor with a glint in his eye and that cheeky smile girls seem to love. "If you play your cards right, I might even cook for you."

Everyone laughs and, for the first time in a long few weeks, so do I. "There, that's much better. Good to see you smiling. We'll go and I'll see you in the morning," Dad says, standing. He kisses me. "Hopefully you can relax tonight. Read over the proposal Connor has been sent and I'm sure everything will seem clearer in the morning. And Connor? Can you send me a copy to read over?"

"Of course."

Callum gives me a huge cuddle and a kiss and whispers in my ear an apology. I shake him away. He hasn't done anything wrong.

"Okay, so it looks like it's just me and you for the rest of the night," Connor says when they leave.

"Looks like it."

"I think you should go run a nice hot bath and do as your dad says and relax. I'll make a start on cooking some dinner."

"Really?" In all the time I've known Connor, I've never known him to cook.

"Yes. Go, before I change my mind."

I stand and walk around to him then kiss him on the cheek, "Thank you." As I leave him alone in my kitchen, I try not to think of the mess he'll make.

Chapter 4

"I HOPE YOU'RE NOT GOING to be much longer." Connor's voice calls out loudly as he stands at the bottom of my stairs with a dish towel in his hand. He looks all domesticated, which is laughable because he rarely does anything for himself.

"Nope," I say, walking down the stairs toward him.

He lifts his head and his eyes follow me with a smile until I'm at the bottom and then he frowns. "Ella McGregor, when I saw you today at the airport, I knew you had lost weight, but fucking hell. The amount you've lost is ridiculous." I glance down my body and I know he's right. I wrap my arms protectively across myself in an attempt to hide from him. I should've worn something else besides this t-shirt and shorts. "While I'm here, I'm making it my job to fatten you up a bit and I'm starting now. I hope you're hungry."

"You know what? I am."

"Glad to hear it." He walks away smiling, and I follow him because whatever he's cooked smells amazing. Let's hope it tastes as good as it smells. In the kitchen, Connor has been busy. I hope he plans on tidying up the mess he's made. I swear he's used every pot and dish I own. It's really quite funny. Under normal circumstances, this mess would freak me out, but my bath has helped me relax, and for the first time in what seems like forever,

I feel like the old me.

And not the one who was completely oblivious twelve weeks ago.

I'm pushing the niggling questions about Donovan to the back of my mind for the time being. Dad is right; I need to put myself first. "This all looks . . . amazing," I say, taking a seat and trying to avoid looking at the mess.

"It tastes even better." He opens the oven and, using the dish towel, takes out a bowl and brings it over to the table where there is already salad and garlic bread and a bottle of wine. He looks at home. Well, my house *has* been home to him these last few years. "Pasta bake with chicken, broccoli, onions, and mushrooms. Real comfort food, according to your dad." I smile because it's one of my favourite meals that Dad makes. Dad isn't the best cook in the world but, then again, my mum was and she insisted on doing all the cooking. This dish is the one my dad likes to cook, and Mum always loved it too.

"If this tastes as good as it smells and looks, you can stay for as long as you want," I say with a smile as he serves some onto my plate.

"About that . . ." He puts the spoon back in the bowl and cocks his head to the side. As he sits studying me, I notice the deep frown lines around his eyes that weren't there earlier. The boyish grin he usually has isn't there. He looks worried and deep in thought and I can take a guess what he's thinking about.

"I know it'll only be for a short time because when Donovan arrives in the country, you can go and stay with him wherever he stays."

"Ella, right now I don't want to see him because I'm so fucking mad with him, but I know my being here will be a constant reminder for you. So I can book into a hotel tomorrow."

"You will do no such thing. It'll be nice having a distraction, not spending all my time on my own. I swear, I'm questioning my sanity on a daily basis."

"You shouldn't be questioning anything, especially about you. He's the one in the wrong. I want answers to all this crap that's swimming around in my head, so I've no idea how you feel. He's really fucked up and you're not the only one who'll need a new agent. I can't work with someone I don't trust or respect and, after what he's done to you, I've lost all that. I might be losing a friend but you're on the verge of losing so much more. I can't believe he left you with nothing."

"I know that," I say with a touch of sadness in my voice. "Okay. For the rest of the night, neither of us is allowed to mention his name." *Because every time I think about him I realise being with Donovan has been the biggest mistake of my life and that breaks my heart.* I've been so stupid. Wasted so much time.

"Deal. Food, wine, proposals and my company. What more could you possibly want?" he teases and I laugh. Connor has always been able to make me laugh and smile.

I shake my head; I've no reply to that. It's strange sitting in my own kitchen eating food that someone else has cooked and it really is tasty.

"Mmm, this is good. Why have you never cooked for me before?"

"I wanted to, believe me." He doesn't need to say anything else. Donovan believes when it comes to cooking and cleaning, it should be a woman's job, regardless of what else they do. He really does have old fashioned values. Why am I only realising this now? *Because he's not around to control my thoughts.* I shake my head.

"I could get used to this."

"Don't get too used to it. My cooking skills are pretty limited, although I'm not too bad when it comes to cleaning, so the mess I've made, I'll clean it up." He knows me well enough to know that I'm a complete clean freak when it comes to my home.

"As long as the mess isn't here in the morning, it will be good enough for me."

"I can do that." As I take a sip of the wine, I don't doubt it. "We have lots to talk about, and I think I should organise a meeting with the casting director to talk over what they're looking for."

"I'll read over your email before I decide to do that."

"Agreed."

"Now can you stop talking and just let me enjoy my food?" He nods. The rest of dinner is eaten in silence. Well, what I can manage. I'm not sure my body knows what's going on. Two proper meals today; it's not used to it.

"I thought you were enjoying it," he says when I put my cutlery down.

"Sorry. Yes, it's lovely, it's just . . ."

"Don't. I don't want to hear it. You've eaten more than I thought you would. Right, go on through to your front room and take our wine glasses. I'll grab my laptop and the rest of the wine." He moves around the island and takes my hand, helping me to my feet. Always the gentleman. As the thought enters my head, I realise that's the way he's always been, and not just with me.

Connor Andrews has never had a bad word printed about him in any tabloids on either side of the Atlantic. His image is very clean cut; always has been. He's never done drugs and I've never seen him pissed. Tipsy, yes, but never drunk. He's dated a few women in the last few years, but claimed they were never anything serious.

There's no big secret, no skeletons hiding in his closet waiting to make an appearance. What you see is what you get with him.

He was born up north, near Inverness, brought up on a farm with his parents. He's worked hard throughout his life to achieve his dreams and his parents made sacrifices to put him through acting school.

"Go. I'll at least put the dishes in the dishwasher." I lift our glasses and wander through the house. It's strange having him here and no Donovan. I expected it would be difficult or at least uncomfortable, but it's not. I feel at ease. Putting the glasses down on the coffee table, I switch on the TV. I've not really bothered with it in weeks. I've tried to be blissfully unaware of what has been going on in the outside world. I start flicking through the channels, avoiding all the news and showbiz channels. There's plenty of time for me to find out what's happening in the showbiz scene and, at the moment, I'm not sure I'm ready to hear it all.

Small steps.

There's not much on TV tonight. I hear Connor's phone ringing and his footsteps walking through the hallway as he answers it. When he enters the room, he switches it to loudspeaker but raises a finger to his mouth, telling me to be quiet. He puts the bottle of wine down beside the glasses and his laptop that he had tucked under his arm.

"So you arrived safely?" Donovan asks. My heart races with anger and frustration hearing his voice for the first time in weeks. I want to scream and shout and I have to cover my mouth stopping me from venting weeks' worth of frustration and anger.

"Yip, and on time."

"How's Ella?" He asks the question but doesn't sound interested in hearing the answer.

I pause, hoping Connor doesn't tell him what I know. "Well, if you would answer her calls you would know she's been ill." I sigh with relief. Connor stands in the middle of the room, eyes set on me. It's not a lie he's telling, he's only withholding some of the truth.

"Oh!" Really? Is that all Donovan has to say?

"Yeah, she's not been out of the house in weeks. Some virus. It's really floored her. You should've been here to look after her, especially when Archie and Callum haven't been in the country either."

"I've been busy." Yeah, right. Busy entertaining half of

Hollywood, I'm sure. Or has it just been Katherine Hunter? I'm glad I asked the last question in my own head because I sound like a jealous bitch.

"It's okay. I'll take care of her until you get here for my premiere. Hopefully she'll be fit and well enough to attend with you."

"About that. I won't be in Scotland for your premiere. Something has come up."

"What the actual fuck? You're meant to be my friend and agent. You should be here. What's so important that its keeping you in L.A?"

"I'm now representing Miss Hunter as well and she has a meeting I need to attend."

"Donovan, I've just told you Ella has been really ill. She still is. Fucking hell. It looks as though she's lost about a stone in weight and all you can say is you won't be home because of Miss Hunter. I think you have your priorities all wrong. The Donovan I know would've been on the first available flight home to take care of his girl. What's changed?" I can hear the anger in Connor's voice as he paces the floor.

"I'm really busy with work. Completely snowed under."

"Yeah, I know, and sorting out meetings for me and Ella in Glasgow should be your concern too, or have you forgotten about that?"

"No, I've not forgotten. There's a few details I need to sort out for you both on this and then you can sign on the dotted line."

Connor stands, shaking his head at me and mouths, 'He's a lying pig.' I can't argue with him on that. He's been lying to me for months. "So when will you be here?"

"I'm not sure. Maybe the week after the premiere. It just depends on what happens over here."

"Donovan, what will I say to Ella? She could do with your support."

"Tell her whatever you like. She'll understand."

"Will she? Because I fucking don't. I don't know what's going on, but you need to sort out your shit and get back home to look after your girlfriend."

"I'll be there as soon as I can. Look, I need to go. I'll give you a call in a few days." Donovan ends the call.

"I swear to God, Ella. Please tell me there is no you and him any longer? Because I'm going to kill him. He must be on drugs. That's the only explanation I have for his behaviour."

"There's no us. I couldn't stay with him after all this, and as you said earlier, the trust has been broken. It was broken the day he left, leaving me with nothing. I'm just hoping my dad and Jonathon don't dig up any more skeletons because I don't want Dad bailing me out constantly because I was stupid."

"Enough." Connor rushes over and sits down beside me. "This is not your fault. He's lied to you and deceived you and he has to pay the price."

"What do you mean?" I ask, looking at him, scared of what I know he's about to say. The one thing I'm unsure of doing.

"I mean you have to go public about what he's done to you."

And there it is.

"No, I can't. I don't want the world knowing this."

"Ella, I get that, but if you do go public, it would destroy his career. He deserves to have everything taken away from him."

"You might be right, but I'm hoping there's another way to do it without involving me."

"Maybe. Now, what are we going to watch?" He must sense my apprehension at our conversation as he changes the subject.

"Here." I hand Connor the remote control. "I don't care as long as it's not a love story."

"I'm sure I can find something."

I top up our glasses and hand Connor his. I take mine and get comfortable on the couch. He flicks through the channels until he lands on an action movie. That'll do for me. He kicks off his shoes as he's done a million times before, making himself at home. I find myself staring at the man beside me. A man who has been a friend to me and continues to be one. There's something different about Connor. Maybe it's because I've heard the conversation with Donovan. I'm not going to think too much about it because, at the moment, I'm relaxed and I don't want that to change.

I turn my attention back to the TV and take a drink. For someone who was meant to be putting Donovan Bell out of my head for tonight, I'm not doing very well. He seems to be everywhere I turn; pictures of the two of us together in this room. Silly things like ornaments he bought.

All this crap has to go.

I try to watch the movie but I'm feeling agitated and also a bit tipsy from the wine. Which isn't a great surprise. I've not had alcohol in weeks. Add that to the small matter that I've not been eating properly. So, of course the alcohol was bound to hit me quicker than usual.

"What's wrong?" Connor asks.

"I'm not really in the mood to watch this."

"Do you want to see the proposal then?"

"Can we do that tomorrow? I think I'll go to bed," I say, standing, but the room spins. Bloody hell. I don't even think I've had two full glasses of wine.

"Here. Take my arm," says Connor, standing up.

"I don't want your help." I take a step away from him, but my body sways.

"You might not want it but you need it."

"Whatever."

We take the stairs slowly. I think Connor's scared I'm going to fall back down. His arm is around my waist, gripping me tightly.

At the top, he stops and opens the first bedroom door. "I'm not sleeping in there," I shout, pulling the door closed. Yes, it's the master bedroom, but I've not spent a night in there since I found out about Donovan.

"Oh. So where are you sleeping?"

"At the back of the house. The last room." He stares at me, puzzled. I know what he's thinking; of all the bedrooms I can pick, I choose the smallest room in the house. "Okay." We walk along the hallway until we reach the end. He opens the door and sighs. I don't blame him. The room is cluttered with most of my things.

He releases me and I throw myself face down on the bed. I'm feeling tired and teary and I want to be alone. "Ella, are you okay?" he asks, his voice full of concern.

I shrug. "I don't know. I honestly don't know anything anymore." My tears fall onto the pillow and I shiver before I feel a blanket being wrapped around me and strong arms holding me.

Chapter 5

"DONOVAN, WHY WOULD YOU DO this to me? To us. Why do you need money so bad?"

"I just do. You wouldn't understand." There's a sadness to his tone, but also an edge.

I look at him and don't recognise the man before me. He's different. His dark eyes stare straight through me, not really seeing me. He's balancing on the edge of being angry and in pain.

"The man I know would've talked to me instead of being deceitful. Going behind my back and robbing from me. Everything I've worked so hard for over the years, you've taken." I sit down, unable to look at him. "If you were in trouble, you could've come to me. I would've tried to help without you stealing from me." He moves across the living room and stands looking out of the large bay windows. "Tell me what's going on. I think after everything I deserve to know, don't you?"

He coughs to clear his throat. "What's to tell? I've fucked up. I got involved in something I shouldn't have and now it's cost me everything."

"How has it cost you?" I ask through my tears. "What have you lost? Because you're still out on the town every other night, splashing someone else's cash. Let's face it, you've spent all of your money and mine. Maybe I should warn whoever it is what type of person you really are; and that's a thief."

He still doesn't turn around to look at me or even offer me an apology.

My emotions are swinging back and forth because I want answers and he's not giving me them. I rise to my feet and march towards him, pulling on his shoulders, roughly forcing him to turn around. "What?" he asks as though I'm the one in the wrong.

"What? You really don't have a clue. I've had to sit back and watch as your car was towed away, and after that I find out you've re-mortgaged my house and re-financed my cars, but not only that, you've somehow managed to empty my bank account. Yet you still manage to stand here in my house and think you've not done anything wrong. You left me with nothing."

"But Daddy will bail you out. I need the money." I have no idea how he manages to say it with a straight face.

I laugh in his face. "You're not getting anything from me."

"Really? Well, two can play this game. I'll make sure you never work in acting again."

"Get out. Get out!" I yell at him and, this time, he laughs. "I don't want you here."

"That maybe so, but I'm afraid you're stuck with me. I'm not going anywhere until I get some money. You owe me."

These dreams—nightmares—are awful. Each night since I found everything out, they've been getting worse. After all this time, it should be better. I sit up in bed, tears running down my face—tears of anger. Donovan Bell might be thousands of miles away from me but he's still managing to get into my head, even when I'm trying to sleep, haunting me. My head is throbbing and my face is wet from tears and sweat. This isn't a good start to the day.

I grab my phone to check the time. It's nine-thirty. I should've been up and ready by now but I'm not and all I want to do is go back to sleep. It was the first I've slept all the way through the night in weeks.

Connor.

He helped me up the stairs and covered me. I felt his arms

around me as I drifted off to sleep. Oh, no. I've made a fool of myself. Now I really do want to slide back down the bed, pull the covers over my head and stay here for the rest of the day.

Whistling from the hallway grabs my attention; it can only be Connor. "Are you decent?" he calls through the door.

Am I decent? I lift the cover and I'm still wearing my shorts and vest. "Yes."

He's got a bottle of water in his hand, along with something else. "Here. Thought you might need these." He hands me the water and some paracetamol. How thoughtful.

"Thanks."

His eyes stop and take me in. "Ella, what's wrong?" His voice is panicked as he sits down on the bed beside me.

"Nothing," I lie.

"Ella McGregor, don't lie to me. Now take a deep breath and tell me why you've been crying."

This isn't fair on him. He shouldn't have to deal with me, but I do as he says. "It was just a dream. A vivid dream about Donovan. He was here, looking for more money. Demanding it, refusing to leave until he got what he wanted. He was unapologetic as to what I've been through."

"I think you need to get out of here. Get out of the house and get some fresh air. Being cooped up here isn't helping you. We could go for a drive after you've spoken to your dad. Grab some lunch somewhere no one will bother us."

"I'm not sure." Deep within, I know he's right, but it's taking these first steps. I'm afraid I'll fail miserably. Self-doubt has lingered within me now for so long.

"You might not be but you need it. Now, go do whatever you women do and come downstairs. Your dad is already here and has lots to tell us." He kisses me on the head before getting off the bed and leaving the room.

I suppose I should move it now as my dad is here to see me.

First important step of today is to get showered and dressed.

Yes, small steps. I'm sure I'm going to keep reminding myself of these on a daily basis until I'm at a place I want to be.

"THERE YOU ARE," Dad says as I enter the kitchen. He stands as I walk toward him and wraps his arms around me. "Are you okay?" he asks. I wonder if Connor has told him about my dream. I look at Connor and he shakes his head in response to my silent question. How does he do that? How does he know what's going on in my head? Especially when I don't. I need to pull myself together because I don't want my dad to be worrying about me constantly.

"Yes. Still a little tired but I'm better than I have been." My eyes dart to Connor. Is he the reason I feel a little better? I'm sure he is part of the reason.

"Well, that's something. Now, sit down. Connor has made some tea and toast. He tells me you didn't eat much last night."

"Connor, you know you shouldn't tell tales," I scold him.

"Is that right?" he teases, handing me a cup of tea. "I did leave out the part where I had to carry you to bed because of the amount of alco . . ."

"Connor!"

"Really?" Dad asks.

"No, but it was funny seeing Ella's reaction." Dad laughs with him and suddenly I feel like it's two against one.

"I don't even think I had two glasses of wine and, yes, I felt it."

"My gorgeous girl, I'm sure you did, what with not sleeping . . ."

"Dad, please. I'll try and take better care of myself."

"I know you will, sweetheart. Now, let's get down to business," he says seriously as Connor takes the seat opposite me. "First things first. I have a new agent for you both. In my opinion, he's the best in the business and not even Donovan Bell comes close to him."

I smile because I already have a feeling who it will be. Trevor Stephens, my dad's agent and closest friend. If I remember correctly, they've been friends for thirty-five years and he's my godfather.

Trevor and my dad are so alike; some people think they're brothers. They have similar features and the same sense of humour and are both possessive of me and Callum.

"Trevor would like to meet you both either separately or together to go through a few things. Now, there may be a few issues with your contracts with Donovan. Ella, yours might be easier to get out of because of what's going on if you decide to take this further, but we can discuss this. There is also the small matter that he hasn't sent you some proposals and scripts for you to look over."

"What do you mean?"

"Well, the soap opera isn't the only thing he's withheld from you. You should've been sent scripts for two separate movies. I've already got Trevor looking into this for you."

"Oh."

"Connor, your contract won't be so easy to get out of because he has fulfilled his end for you."

"If I have to buy my way out of his contract I will because I can't and won't work with someone I don't trust."

"You're a good lad. Trevor and our lawyer will look and see if there is any way around it and get back to you. Now, the proposal for the soap opera is really interesting. I know the programme is going really well. Viewing figures are high and consistent and they are considering putting on an extra show a week. Ella, Trevor will have in his hand the full proposal for you on Monday and I really think you should give it some consideration and then negotiations will start."

"I will." Because one, I want to work, and two, it would mean

I can start supporting myself again.

"You both should because it does come with a great deal and plenty of time off for other projects as and when they come up. I know you have lots to think about. Connor, you maybe more than Ella because it would mean you spending more time here in Scotland and I know how much you love to spread your wings."

"Oh, I don't know. Being here does come with its advantages. Although, if I decide to stay I should probably start looking for my own place. I can't keep staying here with Ella and I hate hotel rooms."

"Well, you can let Trevor know and, if you want to start looking for a house, I'm sure he'll sort that for you. Ella, can you at least eat something?" I completely forgot that's what I was meant to be doing with the conversation going on.

"There," I say, biting into a piece of toast.

"Now, my other news is about Donovan." I try not to cough and splutter. "The fact is, he's broke."

I laugh. "Is that all you have? Even I knew that."

"Ella, all his accounts are in the red. He owes a lot of people money, and not the sort of people you'd want to be associated with. There is some good news for you; after running credit searches, there are no other debts in your name. I was really worried he would've taken out credit cards in your name but he hasn't. So, that's something to be thankful for. Only the cars and this house which I will clear because, well, I don't need an excuse or a reason to keep my daughter safe and I won't justify this to you."

I can't help but smile even though, if I hadn't been so foolish, he wouldn't be bailing me out. Connor tells Dad all about Donovan's phone call last night. "So, that leads me to a question. Ella, are you going to attend Connor's UK premiere?"

"I don't know," I say, glancing between them. "I hadn't given it any thought."

"Well, you should. I'm going so you wouldn't be alone. And I think you need to be seen out and about again. Speculation is mounting because you've been cooped up here and he's across the Atlantic wining and dining every available actress."

"I don't know. I'm not ready to be seen out and about, as you put it, with anybody."

"That's not what I meant and you know it. But you should be going out. There's so much happening here in Scotland, in the industry. Your last public appearance as far as everyone is concerned was for your last movie six months ago. Sweetheart, in this industry, that's a long time."

"I'll think about it," I say.

"You'll do more than think about it. It would mean a lot to me if you came to the premiere. I want you there," Connor says softly, looking directly into my eyes. "And anyway . . ." His tone changes to the playful tone I'm used to hearing. "You and I are going out today, even if I have to drag you kicking and screaming." I turn to my dad for help and he's smiling at Connor. Looks like they really are ganging up on me.

I'm not going to win.

Not with any of them.

Chapter 6

"CAN YOU PLEASE SLOW DOWN and remember this is my car and I love her," I say as Connor takes another bend too quickly. My wee car doesn't know what's going on. It's not used to all this erratic driving.

"Will you just relax?"

"I might if you *slow* down." He laughs at me. Laughs as he takes yet another corner on this country road. I swear, if I survive this little road trip that he insisted taking me on, he might not. I turn away from watching him because it's not doing my blood pressure any good. He hasn't even told me where we're going. I'm sure my dad knew before we left but he wasn't letting on either. He just looked happy that I was going out instead of sitting around my house feeling sorry for myself.

Archie McGregor is the kindest man in the world and I'm so lucky to have him as my dad and friend. He gave me a kiss and whispered in my ear before he left. He's put money into my bank account. I told him I didn't want it, but he said, "It's too late and it's staying there." Of course, I thanked him and told him as soon as I'm back on my feet financially I'll repay him. His reply was to not be so silly. It's made me think he's only doing what any loving dad would do to look out for and protect his family.

But that in itself has got me thinking. I'm fortunate, but what about those who aren't? Those who don't have family and friends to turn to in their hour of need. What do they do?

My dad's question about Connor's premiere has also got me thinking. Maybe I should go, but then again, maybe it's also time for me to read whatever has been written about me and Donovan over the last few weeks. Time for me to deal with and put an end to all the speculation. Because until one of us speaks out, that's all it is.

Why do I get the feeling it will be me speaking out? Maybe Callum is the one I need to speak to. After all, he is a television presenter and reporter. He would give me all the details I need to know and maybe he's the one I should do an exclusive interview with. After all, it would be easier for me talking to my brother than some other presenter or reporter who would only want a pound of flesh.

I can only do that when I'm one hundred and ten percent sure of what I want. And I know I don't want Donovan Bell in my life. What we had is gone. He took that away with his lies and dishonesty. Do I still love him? No. I did, that's why what he's done hurts, because I didn't expect someone I loved to treat me the way he has treated me.

I'm sure as the days pass, it'll get easier but, until then, I'll deal with it the best way I can, with lots of help from family and friends. I should start with dropping Julie a text and arrange to see her before she doesn't want to see me again.

Missing you. I really do need to see you so I can explain x

She replies instantly: About bloody time. How about a night on the town tonight?

Me: Oh, go on. Why not? I'll probably regret my answer but I really want and need to see her.

Julie: Ok, I'll be at yours 8pm and we can get ready together x

Me: See you then x

"What are you smiling about?" Connor asks, parking the car.

I look around and we're at a beach. There's no other cars in this small car park, so it looks like we'll get to go for a peaceful walk in the open air.

"I've just texted Julie. I need to explain why I've not seen her in what feels like forever. She's coming over at eight and dragging me out."

"A night out on the town. Just don't wake me up when you come in. Or maybe I'll need to stay up to help your drunken arse up the stairs again."

"Hey, cheeky." I playfully slap his arm.

"I'm only teasing, but if you're off out for a night on the town, I might phone Callum and see what he's up to. Hopefully it will help clear the air between us."

"Or you could come out with us. Never know, you might even find your perfect girl."

He frowns, getting out of the car, and mumbles something. "What?"

"Nothing," he says, shaking his head. "Come on. Let's go for a walk. The fresh air will do you some good. But if you feel tired, you have to tell me."

"Will you stop fussing? I'm not ill."

"No, you're not, but if you don't start eating properly you soon will be. And two bites from this morning's toast doesn't count. I've kinda promised your dad I would look after you."

"Well, Connor Andrews, you shouldn't make promises you can't keep." I step away from him and start walking toward the beach.

"I'll keep them." His words surprise me, but I do think he'll at least try and keep his promise to my dad.

He's right. Fresh air is what I need. He's behind me only a few paces and I'm glad he brought me out. I carry on walking toward the coastline, small waves splashing against the pebbled sand. I stop when I'm close to the water, close my eyes, and take a deep breath, breathing in the fresh sea air.

I sense him standing beside me before I open my eyes. It's weirdly comforting being around him. "It's nice out here," he says.

"Yes, it is. Thank you."

I turn to face him. He looks serious. "What for?"

"I'm not really sure, if I'm honest. For bringing me out." He nor my dad and brother won't really know what I've been through these last few weeks. Yes, they can all guess, but they won't know the truth. The sleepless nights. The fear I've felt when I had the television on that there would be something on about Donovan. I always ended up switching it off. The panic attacks that I suffered on my own, no one with words of encouragement to help me through it. No one there to hold my hand or hold me in their arms and tell me everything would be okay.

No one was there because I chose not to tell them what was going on in my life. I chose to keep everything bottled up. I tried to deal with it on my own. But how do you deal with all that crap?

I pushed Julie away the farthest because, unlike my dad and Callum, she's been in the country the last few weeks. She suspected something was wrong. Seeing her tonight is my chance to apologise and put things right between us.

It's my chance to get myself back on track.

Now should be about me. Not Donovan bloody Bell.

Connor puts his arm around my waist and I lean in, resting my head on his shoulder. "Hey, don't friends look out for each other? You'd do the same for me. And I know there must be loads going through your head about my friendship with Donovan. Here's where I stand, just in case I haven't made it clear. Our friendship is gone and I wouldn't even know where to begin to try and justify what he's done to you."

"I know. But this must be hard on you."

"Not really. You're my friend and the thought that he's deliberately hurt you isn't something that sits well with me."

"I think I need to see for myself what's been going on with him."

"What do you mean?"

"Well, I saw an article while I was in the hairdressers. He was with Katherine Hunter. So who else has he been out with and in what capacity?"

"Ella, will finding out really make a difference?"

"I don't know, but it might help me to move forward. Put him where he belongs. In my past."

"The only place he deserves to be is in jail for fraud." I turn back, looking out to sea as tears fill my eyes. Connor is right; I know he is. That's what Donovan has done after all; committed a crime. He's right. My dad's right. It seems I'm in the wrong for not wanting this to get out.

I listen to the sound of the water splashing against the rocky shoreline and my thoughts drift to happier times. I've blocked out the noise of the seagulls overhead. There's always been something soothing about being by the sea. I've always loved it. That could be because, as children, Callum and I would spend lots of time with our parents at the beach. Dad's schedule was always busy but, when he was home, his time was devoted to us completely. Mum's time with us was precious. It's only now she's gone that I can truly appreciate how precious it was.

If she was here now, what would she say about everything? If she was here, I know I would've told her at the first sign of trouble. She was always the one I could turn to. She never criticised me or judged me on my decisions, but she was always there when I needed her the most.

The tears that were in my eyes moments ago fall as I think of my mum. She would hate to see me the way I've been. And that's why I'm standing here in the middle of a beach with Connor's arm around me, crying, because part of me knows this whole situation would have hurt my mum.

"Hey. What are these for?" Connor asks, stepping before me.

"My mum." Connor pulls me into a warm embrace and I sink into his arms and let go.

He holds me tighter. "Ella, everything is going to be okay, and your mum, she'd be so proud of you. She'd also be mad at you for this, but she loved you. That was clear."

I let Connor console me because I'm too tired to do anything else. He's the one person I never thought would be by my side. But as he holds me in his arms, all the stress and anxiety I've felt since I found out about Donovan somehow doesn't seem so relevant.

"Ella, you deserve to be happy. You deserve the world. I hate seeing you so sad. Christ, I've only been here a day and it's breaking my heart. You might put a smile on your face, but you're still hiding and, until you make the decision to let it go, it's going to eat away at you."

"I wish it was so easy."

"Life is what you make it. You will come out of this mess with a smile on your face because that's the type of person you are. You're strong and determined but that doesn't mean you can't have this moment of weakness. We all have our weaknesses." He takes hold of my hand and squeezes it and I want to ask him what's his weakness, but I don't. I stare out to sea and I feel better. Better is a good starting place. I can go on and build from this.

I hope.

Chapter 7

CONNOR'S WORDS AS WE STOOD on the beach earlier today have been playing over and over in my mind. Yes, I've always been strong, and now, I'm showing my weakest side. I'm at my most vulnerable and that frightens me.

The world, the media, they've always seen my strong side and I'm not sure I want them to see this side of me.

My tears have long gone and the smile that's been on my face the rest of the day hasn't been painted on. It's real because Connor has made me feel like me again. I feel human. I've laughed so hard at some of the funny things he's said, stupid things that made no sense. It's been a fun filled day, and he took me for lunch. A little quaint place where nobody knew either of us. If they did recognise us, they didn't let on.

Today has been perfect. Just what the doctor would've ordered, if I had been seeing one. Maybe that's something else I should do to get some help with my sleeping and anxiety.

Now though, I'm feeling anxious about going out. I've stopped myself twice from calling Julie and cancelling our night on the town. I know deep down that my fears are unjustified but I can't help it. Self-doubt is hard to overcome. I want to be strong, prove to myself that I'm still me, regardless of the whole Donovan Bell situation.

My bedroom door opens and there stands my best friend, Julie. "Right, you, I have wine," she says, holding up the bottle in her hand and two glasses. I laugh when I look at her feet. How she's managed to walk up the stairs in those heels carrying all that, I'll never know. "And I have my clothes. You, my friend, can tell me what has kept you locked up in this house like a prisoner, ignoring my phone calls and pleading messages. Then I can tell you how stupid you've been and we'll kiss and make up and be friends again."

And, just like that, she marches across the room and plonks herself down on the bed. "Hopefully, whatever you tell me will explain why we are in the smallest room of your house. Oh, and please tell me the handsome Connor Andrews is still single? Although, it will make no difference. He's only ever had eyes for y . . ."

She stops what she's saying and stares at me, thinking of what to say next, but I don't let her speak. "As far as I'm aware he's single."

"Okay, next question. How long is he staying with you?"

"I don't know."

"Okay, I can work with that. There are two hotties downstairs in your kitchen and you're hiding away up here alone." *Who else is downstairs*? I must look puzzled because she answers my unspoken question. "Callum and Connor are sitting in your kitchen having a few beers, laughing and joking."

"I see."

"Who else were you expecting? Donovan, maybe?"

"No. I don't expect to see him any time soon," I say with a heavy feeling in my chest.

She puts her clothes down on the bed, then she proceeds to open the wine and pours it.

"Here's to friends. Even the stupid one who is trying hard to rein in all her emotions, but her best friend can see straight through her." She hands me a glass and I take a deep breath before I take the first sip.

"Yes, I've been stupid and foolish and, yes, I should've seen you before now, especially with everything going on. I've pushed you away when all I've needed was my friends. I'm sorry."

She puts her glass down on the bedside unit. "Ella, everything will be okay. And I'm glad you texted today because, like it or not, I was coming here tonight, regardless. I've been a bad friend leaving you to wallow in your own self-pity. I know I was out of the country for a month, but that still doesn't explain why I didn't push harder to see you. So, for that, I'm sorry." And that is why we're friends. "Now, spill it. Tell me what the great Donovan fucking Bell has done." She's another one that isn't a huge Donovan fan.

I'm beginning to see a pattern. Why the hell did I not see it before?

We sit curled up on my bed, drinking wine, and I tell her everything.

"Okay, I'm slightly gobsmacked by all this. I don't really know what to say to you, except Donovan Bell is an arsehole and obviously doesn't know what's good for him. He's the fool. I hope you're going to drag his name and sorry arse through the gutters. And what about his hunky friend? Why is he staying here? I should march straight back down the stairs and slap him."

"This isn't Connor's fault. He didn't know about any of this until yesterday."

"And you believe him?"

"Yes. He's almost as mad as Callum and my dad. He wants a new agent. Dad is sorting out everything for us."

"So a question; you and Donovan. Are you over?"

"Yes." There's no hesitation in my voice, although I do hear a pang of sadness. I suppose that's to be expected. He's been in my life for the last five years; you don't just get over that in a few days.

Although, I really do wish it was that easy. I need to think about packing his things. That might help me, give me some closure.

"Glad to hear it. It's about time. I always thought you were too good for him and this just proves I was right. Now, it's my mission to get us very drunk tonight and have a good time. Maybe even find you someone you can use for the night to fuck Donovan Bell out of your system." I gasp at her words. That's the last thing I want to do. "All the boring stuff can wait until Monday."

I nod in agreement because, what else can I do? We both laugh. My dear friend certainly has a way with words. We spend the next hour and a half drinking wine and getting ready, doing each other's hair and make-up. All the fun stuff you do with your best friend. Things that have been missing from my life lately.

"There. You look perfect. Not too slutty and not too sophisticated," Julie says as she stands back and takes in my appearance. As I look in the mirror, I see she's done good. The colour in my hair now really stands out with the way it's been curled. My make-up isn't too heavy. And this dress must be the only dress in my wardrobe that actually fits me. The last time I tried it on it was at least a size too small, but not now it's perfect. With its knee length hemline, not too showy at the boobs and low back, it's the perfect little black dress.

"Thanks, and so do you."

"Let's go downstairs. Maybe we can talk Callum and Connor into coming out with us."

"I don't know about that." I know I said that to Connor earlier today, but now I've spent some time with Julie, maybe it would be better if it were just the two of us.

We leave the mess behind and head downstairs. They're in the kitchen. Julie walks on in front of me, and I pause, finding myself watching them. Old memories come flooding back to me of Connor and Donovan sitting there in that same spot. I give myself a shake. Connor lifts his head, slowly running his eyes up my body. I try to turn away, not wanting him to see me, but I can't. His eyes meet mine and a slow smile spreads on his face. His eyes never break contact with mine and, suddenly, I wish I was anywhere but here. I'm transported back to the first time I met Connor.

"You are the most beautiful woman here tonight and I'm honoured to be finally meeting you, Ella McGregor."

I feel the heat in my cheeks as he lifts my hand and raises it to his mouth, placing the softest of kisses on my hand. I shouldn't be standing here allowing another man to flirt with me since I'm on a first date.

"And you are?" I ask as his eyes roam my body. I know who he is, but he doesn't know that.

"Connor Andrews. Hopefully, one day I'll be lucky enough to star alongside you. After dinner, I think I should have the first dance."

Coughing from Donovan interrupts the conversation. "I think you'll find Ella's first dance belongs to me. Ella, I see you've met my friend Connor. Connor; my date."

Poor Connor. I actually feel kinda sorry for him as he stands there, mouth open, glancing between Donovan and me in disbelief.

"Wow, look at you, sis. You look amazing. So much better than you did yesterday." Callum's words stop my train of thought and also stop me turning and walking away. "You having another drink before you head out?"

"I don't think we . . ." |

"Yeah, why not?" Julie interrupts. "But I also think you two should keep us company." What the hell is she playing at? I can't be spotted on a night out with another man or men, even if one is my brother.

"What do you think, Connor? I can think of worse ways to spend my night." Callum's eyes are on Julie as he speaks.

Really, this isn't going to end well.

"Yeah, sure. I did make a promise to your dad that I would look after you and, after last night, maybe it's as well me staying close to you."

My shoulders sag in frustration. Callum laughs and I want to kill them both. Julie's eyes dart between us, wanting to know what the private joke is. Well, I'm sure Connor can fill her in. He's already told my dad and, from the look of it, Callum.

"I think we'll leave the drink and head out now, before I change my mind," I say, taking my phone from my bag and calling a taxi.

"Ella, honey, what's wrong?" Julie asks out of earshot.

"Nothing."

"Doesn't look like nothing. To me it looks as though you've finally seen through Connor's feelings for you."

"What the hell? And you knew? Why didn't you say something before now?"

He has feelings for me? I stand looking into Julie's eyes, hoping that we've all got this wrong, but I only see her conformation. I don't need this. Not now. And not Connor Andrews. But now I pause and think about it, some things make sense. His slip of the tongue yesterday, and Julie upstairs almost said as much.

"Because he and I both knew you were taken, but you're not anymore."

"Bloody hell. He's my friend. But first and foremost, he's been Donovan's friend for years."

"That may be so but he's always wanted you. Now, here we are years later and you're both single. Funny that." I don't know what to say to my best friend.

"I'm not interested in anyone."

"Maybe. But Donovan's been gone months. Do you really think after everything you've found out that he's stayed faithful to you? Come on, Ella. You're not that dumb."

"Cheers for that."

"Only saying it how I see it. You should know me well enough by now."

Yes, I do. Now, why do I feel as though tonight is going to be a disaster? Because everything else in my life has been that way lately. Why should tonight be any different?

I can hear chairs being scraped against my kitchen floor as the guys move. How is it that it's taken Julie and I over an hour to get ready, and that's quick for us, but guys don't even bother? Well, in Connor and Callum's defence, neither of them need to do much. They both look incredible, and I know they'll have ladies falling at their feet.

"Taxi is here," I call through to the kitchen after receiving a text and opening the gates.

"Okay, we're ready," Callum says, looking all smug with himself. I glance toward Julie and back to him and I now realise why; it's written all over his perfect face. He likes her. Really likes her.

"Come on. What are we waiting for?" Julie says, leading the way outside. I stop to switch on the alarm and lock the front door. I gasp when I turn around. Connor is standing there on the steps waiting for me.

"If you'd rather we didn't go with you I can drag your brother to a bar."

"No, don't be silly. As you said, you might need to look after me tonight if I have one too many drinks."

He reaches out and takes my hand. I pause, thinking what this might look like, but let him lead the way to the waiting taxi. We're friends after all.

Chapter 8

BLAZE.

I sigh heavily. Our taxi stops in front of the most exclusive night club and bar in Glasgow. You can only get in here if you're a member. Footballers, their wives, local celebrities; this is where you will find them if they're out on the town.

Why couldn't we go somewhere off the radar? Somewhere there aren't photographers hanging about. I was outvoted when Connor told the driver our destination and the others agreed with him. I was more than happy to go somewhere else.

Why did we have to come to the one place where everyone who's anybody or nobody wants to be seen? There's a couple of photographers standing on the pavement behind a barrier, camera in hand and already snapping in our direction. Security has stepped closer to our taxi.

"I don't know if I can do this," I mutter uneasily, looking away from my friends, closing my eyes, and taking several deep breaths, hoping and praying this doesn't lead to a full blown panic attack.

"You can," says Julie, taking my hand. "And you will. You have us here with you for support." Nagging in the back of my head tells me I can't do this. That I'm not ready to be seen out in public. Not yet.

"Come on, sis. Take a deep breath and this will be easy. All you have to do is smile." Callum makes it sound so easy but my heart is already racing and I'm on the verge of telling the driver to drive away to escape the scrutiny I know I'll face stepping out of this taxi.

Connor sits, regarding me quizzically for a moment. "Ella, do as Callum says. Put that gorgeous smile back on your face. I'm going to count to three, Callum and Julie will get out first, and then I'm going to take your hand and I'll be with you. Right by your side. Okay?" I nod because I see something in his eyes and hear the softness of his voice. "Okay. One. Two. Three." Callum and Julie get out and I watch as my brother puts his arm around her and they pose for a couple of pictures. Connor gets out and holds his hand out and waits for me. I close my eyes briefly to gather my strength before smiling at him and climbing out of the car. Cameras flash from all directions and I can hear my name being called.

Waves of panic sweep over me, but I try to remain calm and composed. Connor, as though sensing how I'm feeling, wraps his arm around my waist and pulls me close to him. The scent of him has a calming effect. I'm not sure why, but it does. My breath catches in my throat as my heart pounds frantically in my chest.

Right here and now, all I want to do is close my eyes and enjoy the feeling of being in his arms. Oh, no. Where the hell did that thought come from?

Callum and Julie stand at the side, waiting. I can see the concern on my brother's face.

"You're doing amazing. Before I forget to say, you look incredible tonight," Connor whispers in my ear as we pose for a picture. I can feel myself blush at his words, and when I turn and look into his dazzling eyes, he's smiling. Oh, God. How is this going to look in tomorrow's newspapers?

"Connor, Ella, it's good to see you out together." I can hear the meaning behind the reporter's words but I choose to ignore them.

Connor, on the other hand, is still looking deep into my eyes and smiling, giving them something else to think about and, no doubt, print. Something else I'm bound to regret tomorrow when I see the headlines.

"Ella, do you have anything to say about the growing speculation surrounding you and Donovan? Do you have some news of your own you'd like to tell us?"

This is what I was dreading; the questions. Callum steps forward. "Tonight, my sister has nothing to say. She wants to enjoy a night out with friends and I'm sure she will give you her story in the coming weeks. Now, we'd like to get inside."

"One more picture of Ella," someone calls out. Connor keeps holding me and we let them get one picture before we're ushered inside by the security.

Still with Connor's arm wrapped around me, I pause inside and let out a long, slow breath. "Now, that was an entrance," a friendly American voice greets us. I recognise the man as Alex Mathews, the American businessman who owns the club. I've met him a few times in L.A. a few years ago, before he married Libby. He was always with Katherine Hunter. I always thought they were a couple; turns out they were only friends.

"Sorry," Callum says apologetically, holding out his hand to him. "This is Connor, Julie, and I know you know my sister."

Alex shakes his hand. "Hi. As long as you're all okay?"

"Yes, we're all fine, thank you," I say.

"Ah, Ella. It's good to see you again, and looking so well." Alex greets me with a kiss on the cheek.

"And you. How are you finding our beautiful country?" I ask him, thinking about how different his life must be here in Scotland compared to living and working in New York.

"I love it here. Michael, can you ensure Miss McGregor and her friends are looked after tonight? Ella, it would be lovely to catch up properly another time when I'm not heading home. Maybe we could do lunch with my wife? I'm sure she'd love to meet you."

"That would be nice. I'll leave my number and you can give me a call and we can arrange that."

"I hope you all enjoy your night."

"Thanks, Alex," I say as he leaves. Michael, Alex's most trusted friend, shows us through the club to what I presume is a VIP area. There's more than a few faces I recognise in here tonight; most of them footballers. That comes as no surprise. Most of them would've had a game today, so this is their down time. We get stopped more than once with people saying hello to Connor and Callum. Connor orders a round of drinks as we sit down.

"I didn't know you knew Alex Mathews," says Connor.

"Yes, we've met a few times at different events. He was always with Katherine Hunter."

"Ah, I forgot there was a bit of history with those two."

"Yes, lots of history and none of it very good. It's such a shame because they grew up together. It's funny how things turn out." Something clicks in my head with my last sentence, bringing me back to my own reality. I've been trying so hard over recent weeks to ignore the truth, but it hasn't done me any good, and now I know I need to face it head on and deal with the consequences.

"Enough of the chit-chat," says Julie as a waitress comes to our table, putting down our drinks. "We're here to enjoy ourselves."

"Julie, you're right. A toast." We raise our glasses and wait for my brother to speak. "To friendship and my sister. The strongest person I know, even though she might not feel like it at the moment."

"Ella and friendship." I smile at my friends and take a drink from the glass of rose wine. My eyes roam the club and I'd say it's almost full, which is as you'd expect for a Saturday night. Music flows and it already looks as though things could be hotting up on the dance floor. There's one couple who catches my eye and I'm thinking they need to get a room. I turn back to my friends and the easy conversation that flows.

"Are you okay?" Connor asks.

"You know what? I'm fine. Actually, I'm better than fine."

"Glad to hear it." He smiles and Callum starts talking to him about football. I really don't see the attraction of it myself. I've never liked it, not really. Don't get me wrong, I can recognise players because of Callum's line of work. He's always doing interviews with them.

Callum told our waitress when she brought over the first round of drinks to keep the drinks flowing at our table. I'm not sure that's such a good idea considering how I was feeling last night with only having two.

"Well, are you going to give in and let your hair down completely tonight?" Julie asks.

"What do you mean?"

"I mean you still look uptight. And given all the attention you've been getting, there's no reason for you to be feeling like that. You look hot tonight and I know you could have your pick of any man, or woman if you fancy a change, in this club tonight."

"Julie!" Connor and Callum look at us, shrugging their shoulders. "There's no way that's happening."

"Oh, I don't know. But you could be onto something because I don't think Connor will let anyone near you."

"Oh, please. I'm not listening to this. I think I need another drink."

"Yes, I agree. We should do shots. Let's have some fun. What do you say, boys? Shots?" Connor grabs the waitress's attention and orders another round of drinks and shots. At this rate, Connor won't be in any fit state to look after me. My heart sinks with my last thought, leaving me with an unexplainable feeling of emptiness.

I lean back in the chair, disappointment fresh in my head. It felt nice today, knowing Connor was concerned enough for me to look after me last night.

With everything else going on in my life, I don't need another complication. It's Michael that brings over the round of drinks this time. Julie picks up the shots and hands them to each of us. "Three. Two. One." With Julie's countdown, we all down the green alcohol.

I shake my head and squeeze my shoulders closer to my ears as the aftertaste lingers in my mouth. Michael laughs as he leaves our table. I hope Julie doesn't plan on drinking more shots tonight, because I'll never keep up.

Yes, I'm a lightweight.

"Right, missy, we're not sitting here all night. Come on and dance with me?" Julie pleads, tugging my hand.

"What, now?"

"Yes. Come on. Let's see what you can do."

"Go on," Callum encourages me. Connor sits quietly, watching my friend pull at my arm. I reluctantly agree and she drags me from our secluded corner seat. We hit the dance floor. I close my eyes for a moment, allowing myself to feel the music; nothing else, just the beat. A rhythm that very quickly pulls me in, making me forget everything else.

When I open my eyes, Julie is moving in time to the beat of the music. "There's my friend. For the first time tonight it looks as though you're right here with me, and enjoying yourself."

"Yes, well there's something about music that helps me forget about the shit-storm that is my life at the moment."

She smiles widely, glancing over my shoulder. "Don't turn around, but a certain someone can't take his eyes from you. From here, his profile looks rugged and sombre. There's a certain sensuality oozing from him as he holds you hostage with those dazzling eyes."

Wow! I have no comeback to that.

"Are you going to dance with him?"

"Julie . . . No. I think I've probably given the media enough to speculate about."

"Oh, I don't know. As your dear mum used to say, 'If they're talking about you, they're leaving someone else alone.'" She spins around, turning her back to me. I risk a glance back to our seats and she's right. Connor's eyes are on me. Callum is speaking to him but it's obvious he's not listening to a word. I turn away back to Julie and carry on dancing.

Dancing and alcohol. Both will keep me occupied for tonight.

One song leads straight into another and another and I find I'm actually having fun. Julie and I shout at each other over the music, reminiscing about past nights out with each new song that starts.

"I'm thirsty," I shout, pulling her with me back to our seats. The guys smile as we sit down. More drinks are already waiting for us, including shots. Tomorrow I'll be useless. I notice Connor is drinking what looks like water. I frown, staring at him.

"What? I've promised I'll look after you and I'm enjoying watching you having fun. There's no way you'll make it up the stairs and into your bed without help and I'll say this now, there'll be no one else helping you into your bed or any other bed."

That's me told.

"You sound like Callum. I have no intention of going anywhere with anyone."

"Three. Two. One!" Julie shouts. I pick up one of the shots and throw it down my throat in one. Oh. My. God; the burn laces my throat. "And another." Julie hands me another shot. We take them quickly. I think my memory about tonight is going to be very blank.

Maybe that will be a good thing as I lift my head and my eyes meet Connor's and, for the first time ever, I see him. Really see him. His brows and eyes are startling against his tanned complexion and dark hair under the lights above. The shadow along his jawline gives him a manly sexuality. As he watches me, I can see touches of humour around his mouth and near his eyes.

I sense a certain amount of arrogance from him and it confuses me. Because I've never thought of him as arrogant.

This isn't good. I take another drink from a glass of wine before standing. I can feel the effects of all this alcohol flowing through my veins. "Julie, come on." I drag my friend onto the dance floor because I'm suddenly uneasy being around Connor.

"What's wrong with you? You couldn't get away from the table quick enough."

"Nothing. Nothing at all."

I glance over my shoulder and, even in this crowded club, his presence is compelling. Why am I only now noticing this?

"Oh, I see why." Yes, she does, and so do I.

Chapter 9

A SENSE OF FAMILIARITY SURROUNDS me and I find myself smiling. That means I'm in my own bed. I open my eyes and give them a moment to adjust to the bright light coming through the bedroom window.

The sun shines brightly in the sky outside and birds are singing, but everything in the house sounds oddly quiet considering Connor is staying here. He can usually be heard whistling or just moving around, but nothing. Does that mean he didn't stay here last night?

Oh God, last night . . .

I try to refresh my memory, but I can't. There's nothing there. The last thing I remember is after the second or was it third round of shots? I must've been in such a state. The last thing I remember is being on the dance floor and looking over my shoulder and seeing Connor watching me. And then absolutely nothing.

How did I get home? Did Connor have to look after me again? Carry my drunken arse up the stairs?

Getting drunk is one thing, but I always remember the events of the night, but this is alien to me. And that's also a good word to describe how I'm feeling. I sit up, the covers lower, and I notice I have no top on. Shit! I lift the covers and see I'm only wearing knickers. What the hell?

I look across this small room and the dress I had on is folded on the dressing table. That tells me someone had to undress me. I cringe. Please let it have been Julie, but if it had been my friend, I'm sure my clothes would be lying in a heap on the floor. So the question is, who put me to bed?

I don't want to get up. I want to lie here, but my head is spinning and I feel as though I want to throw up. I have the hangover from hell. What a way to start a Sunday. I don't even know what time of the day it is. I lean over, looking for my phone, and it's right where I leave it every other night; beside the bed. At least I managed to do that. Picking it up, I see there are a few text messages and a missed call from my dad only thirty minutes ago. It's one p.m. I'll call him back as soon as I've showered and grabbed myself a strong black coffee.

Julie has texted. You call me as soon as you're in the land of the living. The sooner the better!!!

Oh, no. What have I done? I'm not sure I want to know.

Everyone can wait until I'm showered. I climb out of bed and stand on unsteady legs. My entire body shakes and the room spins.

Bloody hell, I'm never drinking again.

PULLING MY T-SHIRT over my head, I at least look clean. I still feel like crap, but that's to be expected when you have next to no memory of the night before. My first task of the day is done. Now time for the second. I need to go downstairs and make myself a coffee.

The house is still quiet; no sound of movement or life. As I pass Connor's bedroom, the door is open. I peak in and he's not there, but his bed is made. He must be downstairs. I hope I haven't made a complete arse of myself.

In the kitchen, there's no sign of Connor, but there are two mugs and plates sitting near the sink and the kettle is still warm.

So, Connor and who else? And where are they now?

I switch the kettle on and wander over to the patio doors and open them. Warm air hits me from outside. I step out onto the deck and breathe in. It's a gorgeous day. A day that should be made the most of because we don't get many. When I make my coffee, I'm going to grab a pair of sunglasses and come out here to sit for a bit. I hear the kettle and go back inside.

I make my coffee, help myself to a couple of chocolate biscuits, and head back outside with my sunglasses because it's too bright for my eyes.

It seems funny sitting out here with my coffee with a hangover, especially when the last time I was sitting here only a few days ago, I was in floods of tears, wondering what the hell I was going to do. Wondering how I was going to make ends meet. But even feeling the way I do today, everything is so much better.

A wise woman said to me when I was still a child that, 'There is always something good, even in a bad situation. It's just about looking in the right places.' I take a deep breath and stare out; my mum was right. She was right about most things, although I'm not sure she would find something good about Donovan and the current situation.

Time to call my dad. The phone rings a few times before he answers. "Afternoon," I say, surprising myself with how cheery I sound.

"Well, you sound much better. Did you have a good night?"

"What I can remember of it."

"Ella . . ."

"Don't. It was a one off. I don't make a habit of getting drunk."

"No, you don't. Are your brother and Connor at yours yet?"

"No, why?"

"They left not long ago. They had been out for a run and stopped in here, so they should be with you soon."

"Ah, okay." That will explain the mugs and plates. They've

obviously had some breakfast. I wonder if Callum stayed here last night.

"Now, what I was calling you for . . . I'm glad you made the effort to go out last night. Can you imagine my surprise when I picked up this morning's papers to see my daughter on the front page looking so much better?"

"What? Oh, no. I presume I'm with Connor?" My thoughts are of our arrival at Blaze last night.

"Yes and, you know what? I'm glad. You've been hiding away for far too long because of that waste of space, so why shouldn't you be out and about with someone?"

"Dad . . . Connor is my friend." I knew this was bound to happen but I did hope the pictures wouldn't have made today's papers. I want some peace. Tomorrow would've been time enough. This means Donovan will see these pictures sooner too. Or maybe he's just not that interested in what I'm doing.

"Yes, I know he is, but I can h. . . . Look, the pictures will do what they're meant to do and that is letting the world see you're not hiding. Because, at the moment, everyone thinks you're doing that because Donovan has been cheating on you."

"And has he?"

"Sweetheart, you need to decide that for yourself. Will it make any difference to you now if he has or hasn't?"

Will it? I pause briefly before answering. "No. Our relationship was over the day he left me with all these problems. Maybe it was over long before he left."

"So, what are you doing the rest of the day?"

"Nothing. I have a hangover."

"What about going out for dinner with your old man?"

"Just the two of us?"

"Yes."

"You, old man, have a date." I can hear the amusement in his voice as he tells me what time he'll pick me up before we end our call. Two nights out in a row. Nothing like causing speculation. It'll be nice to spend time with my dad. Since Mum died, I've seen each day with my dad as a blessing and we're really close. Or rather, we were, until I decided to keep the situation with Donovan from him. I know Dad won't hold it against me.

Putting my feet up on the opposite chair, I take a drink of my coffee before I even think about calling Julie. I bet she only wanted to tell me all about today's papers. Talking from inside the house grabs my attention. It must be my brother and Connor. I stay where I am. If they want me, they can come outside. I'm relaxed and comfortable sitting in the sunshine, and moving would take so much effort on my part.

After a few minutes, I hear their footsteps on the deck. "Well, it looks like someone has a hangover," Callum says with a laugh, pulling the chair my feet are on and sitting down.

"Hey! I was comfortable."

"Yeah? You also looked comfortable when I tried to wake you to come for a run with us."

I laugh and almost spit my coffee all over him. "Yeah, even if I had woken up that was *never* going to happen." I put my coffee down and lean back in my chair. *Going for a run.* Is my brother mad after the amount I had to drink last night? Movement at the side of me catches my attention and, when I turn to look, I'm so glad my sunglasses are still on. He stands there looking devilishly handsome. Everything about Connor Andrews is in proportion. My hidden eyes travel the length of his body. His mouth curves into an unconscious smile as he watches me with deep brooding eyes; he knows what I'm doing.

Connor moves toward the table, shirtless. His t-shirt is in one hand and coffee cup in the other. His shorts are sitting low-ish on his hips, giving me a perfect view.

Oh. Dear. Lord.

I turn away quickly before my face reddens. "Did you enjoy

your run?" I ask.

"Yip. You should've joined us," says Connor, taking a seat. His hair is damp and beads of sweat line his forehead. "It would've done you the world of good."

"Eh, I don't think so. What are the plans today?" I ask, changing the subject. Even on a good day, I don't go running. It's not something I enjoy. But maybe I should . . .

"Not sure yet. We wanted to see what you were doing," Callum says.

"I'm going to dinner later with Dad, but until then I'm doing nothing but sitting on my arse."

"So you've spoken to him?" I nod. "Good. I can show you this then." Connor hands me a newspaper he was hiding under his sweaty t-shirt.

I study the front page picture and I don't know what to say. I look okay, considering everything, but what's holding my attention is Connor. The look in his eye as he looks at me while my attention is focused on whoever was taking the picture. I stare at the picture for a few long drawn out moments as silence fills the air around us.

Julie is right. This has to be the reason she wants to talk.

Should I even read the story that goes with the picture? I should find out what is being said about me.

Ella McGregor has finally made her first public appearance since speculation began about the trouble in her relationship with Donovan Bell. She was enjoying a night out with her brother and friends at Glasgow's exclusive Blaze nightclub, owned by the wealthy American Alexander Mathews.

Callum McGregor even hinted that his sister would be giving an interview in the coming weeks to end the speculation surrounding her and Mr Bell.

Miss McGregor may have some news of her own to share. As our picture shows Miss McGregor looked very comfortable and relaxed in the arms of Donovan's best friend, Scottish actor Connor Andrews.

Both Mr Andrews and Miss McGregor looked happy in each other's company. Sources close to the couple tell us they will be starring in a movie together and our very own Scottish soap opera wants both actors to join the cast.

I stop reading because my eyes can't focus on the words. They keep drifting to the picture of me and Connor.

"Come on, sis. Say something."

I lift my head and avoid looking at Connor, "What do you want me to say?"

"I don't know, but I thought you would have something to say. You must really have a hangover." He laughs.

"Don't talk to me about hangovers. I don't even remember coming home."

"I'm not surprised." I know I need to turn to his voice but I don't want to. "Ella?"

"What?" I snap, finally turning to face him.

"You know what? Forget it. Maybe you should go and lie back down so you're in a better mood when you go out with your dad." Connor turns and walks back inside.

"What the hell is wrong with you?"

I take my sunglasses off and look at my brother, studying his expression for a moment. "Callum, is there anything you'd like to tell me?" I ask him, but I already know he's keeping something from me and probably has been for some time. Why am I the last to know? Who else knew Connor has feelings for me?

My brother squirms under my gaze. He leans forward in the chair. "I can't lie to you. Connor cares about you, always has, and I'm sure always will. Does Donovan know? I'm sure he does, although it's never been spoken about. I've seen the look of sadness and regret in his eyes each time he's had to look at you and Donovan together over the years."

So not only did my best friend know, but Callum too.

"Ella, I know you have a shit tonne of stuff going on and you might think those sunglasses hid the shocked look on your face when you saw that picture of you both, but it didn't. You finally saw what everyone else sees when you two are together. I have no idea what, if anything, you'll do, but the one thing I know is that Connor Andrews loves you but he will always be your friend, if that's all you want from him. Right now, we all want you to get your life back on the track you want it to be. I want my sister back. The one I had fun with last night. The one who was always strong and independent. Not the one who has let a man dictate her life, and don't try and deny it because we both know he's done that."

A tear slips down my face and Callum moves. He sits beside me and wraps his arm around me. I rest my head on his shoulder. "I wish Mum was here with us."

"So do I. Ssh, come on. Everything in your life is going to work out the way it's meant to," he tells me, but I'm not so sure. "How about I ask Connor to come and stay with me? Give you some space."

"I don't know." I'm not prepared to admit that I enjoy him being here. But now I know he has feelings for me, it seems wrong. I'm being selfish wanting to have him here with me, especially when I'm not sure I have anything to offer him.

Now I feel as though five years ago I made the wrong decision when Donovan and I started dating. The first night I met Connor was my first date with Donovan and, yes, Connor has flirted with me whenever he was around me, but that all stopped when my relationship with Donovan became serious and very public.

Suddenly, my life has gotten a lot more complicated.

Am I strong enough to take everything that life has thrown my way?

Chapter 10

"SO WHAT ARE YOU GOING to do about Connor's premiere?" Julie asks as we sit having lunch in my back garden. It's another warm day, even though it's cloudy. The forecast is for rain and a thunderstorm so we're making the most of it being dry.

"It's only two days away. I can't not go. That wouldn't be fair to him. He's always been there for me over the years, even if I am only noticing it now. But all this attention I'm receiving at the moment, it's not what I want." Sunday's newspapers and today's have all run with stories on me. Today's featured a picture of me and Dad from last night when we went for dinner and the story written was still full of speculation about me and Donovan, which is funny as there is no me and him.

"Ella, this is the lifestyle you chose. You could've picked some other career, but you wanted to be an actress. You wanted all the fame, even from a really young age. And do you know what? You are one of the biggest actresses to come out of Scotland. You are up there with the best in the industry and you deserve to be. You are one of a kind with a big heart. And you should be at Connor's premiere because the world needs to know you aren't hiding behind closed doors. The big question that I'm sure everyone will be dying to know is will you be on his arm or not?"

"Julie! He's not asked in that way." I didn't sleep well last night.

I'd like to put it down to my hangover, but I couldn't get Connor out of my mind after talking to my brother and then Julie on the phone yesterday afternoon. Julie told me that it was Connor that put me to bed on Saturday night, so I've avoided him since I found out. He saw me practically naked.

"And if he did, what would you say?"

I pause, thinking about her question. Would I? I'm not sure. It feels too soon and a massive risk to our friendship. "Julie, you're putting me on the spot."

"Yes, but better me than Connor. You know, I'm going to the premiere too."

"Well, we can go together then?"

"Maybe." *Maybe.* What sort of an answer is that from my best friend? "Ella, come on. It's time to be honest with yourself and put Donovan Bell where he belongs, in the past. Because, let's face it, that's what he's done with your relationship. You and I both know he's not given you a thought since the day he left."

She has a point. Even when he was on the phone to Connor, I never heard any regret in his voice about not being here. There was nothing to suggest that he even cared for me.

Julie has been here since nine this morning, when I called her wanting someone to be with me when I decided to finally look through every article that has been written about me and Donovan in all our weeks apart. I needed her and she didn't hesitate. She's even helped me in clearing away some pictures of the two of us together and all his belongings are now packed into boxes and in the garage.

I sat reading article after article and, although none of them actually confirmed he has been cheating on me, I know deep within my heart he has. Can I even call it cheating when he turned and walked away? He's been seen out on the town with a number of actresses, and it seems he and Katherine Hunter are very close. They've been seen together on a number of occasions, each time looking cosier than the last. She's the reason he's still in L.A and not here. I thought I would be sad at admitting to myself what he's been doing to me, but in all honesty, I couldn't care. All the damage has already been done and I'm trying to deal with it and move on.

But I still want answers from him. I need to know why he's done what he's done. Dad has hinted that he's in trouble with some unsavoury characters. Is he doing drugs? Or maybe gambling. Is that why he owes a lot of people money? I shouldn't be thinking about Donovan. He doesn't deserve my energy and that's what I'm wasting every time I think about him.

"I will. I promise. Callum is getting an exclusive interview with me. It will be aired sometime during the week."

"That's a start, but have you made up your mind about Donovan?"

"Yes. I know I need to put my story out there but it's not going to be easy for me. Because to me, it means I've fucked up. I've let a man walk over me and that isn't sitting well with me."

"Ella, you need to stop this. What he's done is wrong and you know it. He's committed a crime. More than one. You've had to deal with this on your own, but it's time for you to take back. Yes, you probably won't get anything from him, but he should pay the price for the crimes he's committed, and if that means he loses clients, then so be it."

This is what I'm going to do in my interview. I'm sure it will be easier because it will be my brother asking the questions. He'll be a bit more understanding than most reporters.

"Come on. Lots of good things are happening too. You've got some of the money back in your personal account."

That's true. I took a phone call from my bank manager a short time ago, telling me the money was back in my account because I had reported fraudulent activity. With the joint account, there was nothing that could be done because both our names were on it. But I'm already feeling relieved.

"Now, let's get back to what we were discussing."

"Okay, I'm going to the premiere of Connor's movie along with you, Callum, and my dad. And then I'm going to refocus on my career because I need to do that for me. No one else."

"That sounds like a very good idea."

Yes, it does, and today almost everything in my life seems clearer. I hear footsteps in the kitchen which means my Dad and Connor are back. Connor had a meeting with Trevor first thing this morning and I hope everything went well for him. Dad and I went to see Trevor last night after our dinner and he is going to be my new agent. I now need to issue a statement breaking all professional ties with Donovan, which I'm sure by now Donovan is expecting.

"Hi, you two," I say, turning. "How did it go?" I try to avoid looking at Connor because I'm still embarrassed about the fact that it was him who put me to bed. If only I had worn a bra on Saturday night, then he wouldn't have seen anything.

They sit down. "Well, I have a new agent. It's costing me to get out of my contract with Donovan, but we already knew that. So, all is good. He should find out today whenever he checks his emails." Connor looks really happy. I wonder what Donovan will make of this new development. As soon as he opens the email from Trevor, he'll know that I know what he's done. I shiver. I just can't help myself.

"Sweetheart, what's wrong?" Dad asks.

"I need to tell my story before Donovan decides to make up some garbage about me, because, let's face it, after everything else he's done, I wouldn't put it past him."

Dad picks up his phone and I watch as he types out a message. "You're right, Ella, you do. I've messaged Callum and Trevor. Trevor should be here when you do and I'm sure Callum can fit you into his schedule today."

"Really?" *Today.* I'm not sure I can do this.

"Yes." Of course he can. This is my brother.

"Oh, if you're going to give an exclusive interview, we should go and start preparing," Julie says. She's already told me on more than one occasion today how tired I look.

"Dad, will you be here for this too?"

"Yes." Dad's phone buzzes in his hand. He looks at the message. "Your brother and a camera man will be here in the next hour and a half. Does that give you time?"

Dad's question is asked to me, but it's Julie who answers, "Of course she'll be ready." She stands, taking my hand, and pulls me to my feet. Dad laughs with a warm smile and Connor, well, I can't quite place the look that crosses his face. He looks a little nervous, to be honest.

"If they get here before you come downstairs, which room will I get them to set up in?"

"The front room," I call out as I'm pulled through the house. Julie is a woman on a mission and not one to be messed with.

"Right, lady. You need to shower, wash your hair, and shave."

"Excuse me?"

"Legs, underarms, and anywhere else that needs a tidy up."

I laugh at her. "Because I'm going to be flashing hairy parts of my body to the camera man? Anyway, it's all done. You do remember we had a night out?"

"Yes, I remember. Now, go and get in that shower and I'll pick you something comfortable yet sexy to wear."

I shake my head, leaving her behind. Comfortable and sexy; she's got to be kidding. I have no idea what the hell she'll have me wearing, but I'm confident she won't make me look like a hooker.

"YOU LOOK PERFECT," Julie says, tucking a strand of hair back in place.

"Do you think so?" I look in the mirror. Tight-fitting light blue jeans hug my long lean legs, and a white vest top with a cardigan completes the look. A wee bit of cleavage on show, but the cardigan makes me look relaxed. I hate to admit it, but she's right. This is an outfit I would probably pick to go shopping; it's relaxed and comfortable, and teamed with a pair of heels, it looks amazing.

Julie has done a fab job with my hair and make-up. The soft bounce in my hair lifts the look of the subtle make-up.

I don't know why she doesn't consider going for a job on a set instead of working in a salon. She's brilliant at what she does.

"Yes, I think so, and I also know Callum is waiting for you downstairs. Come on. Let's do this."

I take a deep breath, square my shoulders back, and leave the bedroom, following Julie downstairs. I hear voices in the front room and, putting a smile on my face, I enter to see my dad, Trevor, Connor, Callum, and Stephen, the camera man. A full house. I'm glad it's Stephen. Of all the guys Callum works with, he's the nicest. They stop talking when I enter.

"Don't stop on my account."

"It's okay, sis, we won't. Are you sure you're ready for this?"

Everyone's eyes are on me, waiting and watching. "Yes. Come on. Let's get this done."

"That's my girl." Dad kisses me on the head and moves to the other side of the room beside Connor and Julie. Trevor gives me a few instructions and tells me if I'm unsure of any of the questions Callum asks, I've just to look at him for direction.

God, I'm nervous. I've never been nervous for an interview in my life before.

I sit down and Stephen and Callum start fussing and fluff the cushions around me. When they are satisfied, Callum sits at the other end of the sofa. I risk a glance over the room and Connor looks worried. An unwelcome tension stretches between us and this is my fault because I've been avoiding him to a certain extent. We need to sort this out. He smiles and I turn back to Callum.

"Ready?" he asks. I nod. Stephen signals that he's starting to record. "Ella, thank you for giving us your exclusive interview. So, we are here today, in your home, to bring an end to all the speculation surrounding you and Donovan Bell."

"Okay, first things first. My relationship with Donovan has been over for the last three months."

"Why haven't you spoken up before now? Why leave the showbiz world thinking you were still a couple?"

"Truthfully?" Callum nods and I find myself taking a deep breath. "Because some things have happened that have left me embarrassed. You see, Donovan Bell is a liar and a criminal. He has fraudulently obtained money by re-mortgaging my house and cars, and clearing all my bank accounts."

"Ella, you have nothing to be embarrassed about. Now, where does that leave your professional relationship with Donovan Bell?"

"There have been a few issues with my contract. Donovan hasn't kept up his end of the contract so the contract is nil and void. From today, I have a new agent. Trevor Stephens will be handling business for me. Not only is Trevor a close family friend, but he's still my father's agent, so that tells me he's still one, if not the best in the business."

My eyes find Trevor and I know I've said the right thing; he's smiling. If I keep my answers short and to the point, I'll get through this interview.

The interview continues for another half hour and we cover all topics from Donovan to what is next for me. According to Callum, my name has been linked with a new movie in the last two weeks. I couldn't confirm or deny it as I know nothing about it. Although, I did stress that if anyone watching had sent a script to Donovan, they should now drop an email to Trevor.

We're just about to wrap up when Callum asks the one

question I thought as my brother he would stay clear of. "Ella, the showbiz world will want to know . . . is there another man in your life?"

I silently curse my brother, but find my eyes drifting across the room until they meet Connor's. This is stupid. Why has he even asked that question? What is he playing at? "Callum, I'm sure you will be one of the first to find out when there is another man in my life and then you have my full permission to share my news with the world."

Stephen turns the camera off and steps in front of it. "You did great, Ella," he says, before turning to my brother. I'm relieved that I've done it, yet scared at how I will be perceived once it's aired. As I listen to Stephen and Callum talking, that could be as soon as one of the late shows tonight both here and then in the States. Providing Stephen gets back to the studio now to see if it needs editing.

"Sweetheart, that was perfect. Wasn't it, Trevor?"

"Yes. Ella, I'll be in touch with you in a few days once I have negotiated the contract with TV company. Now, Archie, we should get going." I smile as I think of where they're going. Since Mum died, Trevor's wife, Betty, has always cooked for Dad on a Monday night. Actually, she'd probably cook for him and us most nights if we would let her. I give them both a kiss and say goodbye.

"Sis, I'm going to go back to the studio with Stephen and make sure that you'll be happy with the final edit." Stephen is all packed up and ready to leave. I thank them although I give my brother a bit of a hard time for his last question. He only shrugs his shoulder, his eyes darting back and forth to Connor before leaving. Why do I get the feeling everyone is trying to push us together?

I stand in the middle of the room and turn toward Connor. Julie is talking to him but he's not listening. He stands just to the side of the fireplace and his hooded eyes are on me. Suddenly, I have a vision in my head of Christmas. Not one from the past. One where he's standing where he is with a glass of wine in his hand and there's no one else in the house but the two of us.

This is crazy.

I pull my drifting thoughts back to the present.

There's a shift in the air between us. I can no longer avoid him; we have to talk, although from the seductive way he's looking at me, he doesn't want to talk, and if I'm honest with myself, I don't want to talk either. His eyes rake boldly over my body, dropping from my eyes to my shoulders then slowly lingering on my breasts.

My heart is pounding in an erratic rhythm deep within my chest. He's near but yet still feels so far away. My body feels heavy and weak under his intense gaze. An undeniable magnetism is silently building between us, completely unknown to Julie who is still rambling on. She finally stops talking and her eyes dart between us. She takes a few steps toward me and smiles. "I'll go and leave you to sort this out."

Chapter 11

THIS IS CONNOR, MY FRIEND. The guy with the boy-next-door kinda handsome look. His dark brown hair sits perfectly given the small fact that his hands have drifted through it on more than one occasion during my interview with Callum. His dark eyes are intense. My head has been in turmoil about my growing feelings for him and I don't know what to do. It's been made more complicated knowing that, for the last five years, he's hidden his feelings for me.

We have a friendship, and it works, or so I thought.

Have the last five years of my life that I've wasted all been a lie? I hope not.

I'm hesitant to take the first steps but, in the back of my mind, something is telling me I have to be the one to make the move. He needs and wants to know this is what I want.

What is bringing us together now after all these years? The fact that I'm single may have something to do with it. My thoughts drift back to our very first meeting, and yes, there was no denying I was attracted to him, but who wouldn't be? If Donovan and I hadn't got together, Connor is just my type.

Suddenly, moments that we've been in each other's company, dancing at events with his arms securely around my waist, feel like stolen moments in time. Is that what others think? Is that what Donovan thought?

Without thinking, my legs move, his eyes are fixated on me with each step bringing us closer together. Nerves fill me because I'm scared. Scared of rejection. Scared of being judged.

"Ella!" Something about the way he says my name causes my feet to falter. I'm right in front of him. I can feel his breath against my skin. Close enough for me to wrap my arms around him and want him to hold me.

I take one last step and my body touches his. My breasts press against his firm chest, leaving me aching and wanting. Craving him. I know I could be about to make the second biggest mistake of my life, but here and now, I don't care. Everything from this moment onwards will change.

I want Connor Andrews.

I need to feel him.

I need to lose myself to him.

I drop my eyes from his, but his soft, warm hand touches my chin and tilts my head so, once again, I'm staring back into his dark brown eyes. He leans forward and presses his lips to mine, not giving me another second to think about what this means. Not giving me another minute to back out. My body is tense against him.

I give in to my feelings. I slide my hands up his chest as his hands hold my face firmly in place where he wants it. His tongue slips between my legs and my breath catches; all I can do is moan softly into his mouth.

His strong hands stroke the sides of my face as we sink deeper into the kiss. A kiss I never want to end. My body finally melts against his, my hands roaming all over his muscular chest, feeling him, when he suddenly pulls his lips away from mine, leaving me breathless and uncertain.

"Ella." His voice is laced with pain as he says my name and I can't work out why. "If this isn't what you want, tell me now," he says, closing his eyes briefly. I hear the pain in his tone and I hate that I'm the cause.

His hands tense as he rests them on my shoulders, waiting for my answer. This isn't fair. I can't leave him not knowing. "Connor, I want this."

He moves his hands under my arms, lifting me up. Instinctively, I wrap my legs around his waist. The smile on his face tells me I've said what he was waiting to hear. He strides with purpose through the house and up the stairs, along the hallway until he stands before his bedroom door.

He pauses.

"Connor . . ."

He stares at me for a second, eyes locked on mine. This time his body is tense as he seems deep in thought. Whatever thoughts were going through his head, he shakes them off and pushes the bedroom door open and walks closer to the bed.

When he stops, I jump from his hold. He stands before me, his eyes on mine as I start to undress. The cardigan and top both go. They lie on the floor in a heap. I loosen my jeans, leaving them open, so they hang on my hips as I kick off my heels. I stand three inches shorter than I was mere moments ago. Still, his eyes never leave my face, brimming with desire. They never wander, to take in what I'm giving him.

I remove my jeans and reach my hands around my back and unhook my bra, allowing it to fall to the floor where it joins the rest of my clothes. I'm now standing before him in only my underwear.

He reaches out his hands, pulling my body into his. "You won't change your mind this time?" His question startles me and I try to pull back, but he holds me tighter. "You really don't remember?" He chuckles lightly and I shake my head because I have no idea what he's talking about.

With one hand now at the nape of my neck and the other

gripping me tightly at the waist, my thoughts are lost as his lips find mine in a frenzy of lust. Desire unfurls as our lips mesh together; tongues taste and tease.

Shit! A really strange thought, or is it a memory from Saturday night, flashes through my head, of me standing in front of him in my bedroom as I let my dress slip down my body onto the floor.

I pull back and stare into his eyes. "Oh, no."

"Oh, yes, but I couldn't allow it to happen, even if you had been prepared to take the next step. I need you to remember every last detail of our time together. It broke me."

"You walked away from me?"

"Yes and no. I promised you I would look after you and that's what I did until you were fast asleep, and only then did I walk away. I don't regret leaving you alone the other night; it was the right thing to do. But I won't regret this happening now because it's meant to be." His voice is strong and even. No hesitation and no regrets. Not from him, only me.

"Don't overthink this," he says, lowering his lips back to mine. I don't. Again, I'm lost in the feeling of his lips and tongue against mine. The only thought that enters my head is how quickly can I get him naked?

I work my hands slowly across his back, feeling his breathing quicken against my fingertips. Then around his waist until I reach for the waistband of his jeans. I fumble with the buttons before he stops. His chuckle is deep and I can't help but giggle as I drag my mouth from his. "I'll get these and this," he says as he reaches for the hem of his t-shirt and pulls it up and over his head, leaving me drooling as I take him in.

This is stupid. This is a part of his body I've seen a million times before.

I try keeping my eyes on his as he unfastens the first button on his jeans, but it's hard; all I want to do is sneak a peek. I don't though. I keep my focus straight ahead until he reaches down and removes his jeans.

He's back before me, his eyes dark and clouded, then his lips press fiercely on mine. I press my hands against his chest before drawing them down his body, feeling every muscle tighten and relax under my touch, all the way down to the perfectly formed V until I reach the waistband of his boxers. My nails scrape along his lower abs and his breath hisses.

He grabs my hair, wrapping it around his fist, pulling my body closer to his. I gasp, feeling his impressive erection pushing against my stomach. He tilts my chin and I sigh as his lips leave mine and, slowly, he places the softest of kisses along my jawline.

"You, Ella McGregor, are the most beautiful woman in the world," he murmurs against my neck as his free hand glides down my skin, finding my breast. My head rolls back and my eyes close as his lips descend.

I gasp out loud when the warmth of his mouth covers my breast. Sensations flood me, leaving my body dripping in a pool of desire as he sucks harder on my nipple. *Bloody hell.* The ache that has been simmering through my body intensifies and all I want is for him to lower me to the bed, remove our underwear, and slide deep inside me.

His teeth graze against my nipple as he slowly releases it. My insides are in turmoil with desire that is bursting to release. He smirks as though sensing how I'm feeling. He picks me up and gently lowers me to the bed. So, maybe I am getting exactly what I want.

Crawling slowly up the bed, I allow myself to watch him. He grabs hold of my arms, pinning my wrists on the bed above my head. I wriggle against his hold but he's strong. I'm really no match for him.

With our eyes on each other, he leans down and teases my lips with his. He licks along my bottom lip with his tongue as his erection presses against me, exactly where I want it to be.

He sits up on his knees, freeing my arms. "Ella, do you care to share what you're smiling about."

"No," I reply quickly and breathlessly.

"Oh, I can hazard a guess." He lays his fingers on my stomach and gently starts drawing circles against my skin, around and around. The motion already has me gripping the bed sheets beneath me. His fingers travel further south and I expect to feel them at the waistband of my knickers, but I don't. Instead, they glide over the fabric, tracing back and forth.

"Was this what you wanted?"

"No."

"So, tell me what you want, because until you do, I won't know."

"Connor . . ." His name rolls from my lips as he continues to tease me. "Please!"

"Please what?"

"I want you. All of you."

He tilts his head from side-to-side watching me. Everything about him has me wanting more. "I know that." I gasp at his boldness. "But I think I should have some fun first."

I'm about to ask what he means when cool air hits my heated flesh as he pushes my knickers to the side. I cry out when his mouth makes contact. His fingers part my flesh and slip inside me and his tongue glides up and down. All sorts of sensations course through my body and I'm trying to hold back.

I moan loudly as soon as his fingers hit that sweet spot inside me that sets a fire ablaze. He continues teasing all my senses, licking and rubbing, and it all causes the right amount of friction that sets off my undeniable crash.

My eyes close tightly as the intensity rises. His name falls from my lips as I ride out the orgasm he's taking from my body. His mouth is still buried between my lips, licking and sucking until it's all too much to bear.

I'm still spinning out of control when I feel him slide back up my body. Then he's there, his mouth on mine, tongue parting my lips and delving deep inside. He's teasing and I'm tasting. I moan.

He takes my head in his hands, controlling our kiss. And I let him. I hold nothing back until he pulls away and I'm left breathlessly staring into his eyes and wanting more. "Starters are always very teasing, don't you think?"

I have no answer to that. He removes his body from mine. With his hands on the waistband of my knickers, he removes them and stands. His eyes roam my body before he lowers and removes his boxers. His eyes are still on me. I feel them but my eyes are fixed on the impressive sight before me.

Closing my eyes, I give myself a shake before opening them again. He stands at the edge of the bed, full of confidence. There's a cocky smirk on his face as he watches my reaction, amusement hidden just behind his lustful eyes.

He stands, staring, maybe thinking about what's about to happen. One of two things will happen; this will either be slow and sensual or fast and hard. If he gives me the option, I want fast and hard.

He grabs my legs, pulling me down the bed until they hang off the end. Looks like I'm about to get my way.

I'm completely unashamed as my eyes fall over his body to the part I want to become acquainted with. I watch, envious, as he draws his hand back and forth along his length several times. My breath catches in my throat. I want to be the one doing that, giving him pleasure. With a smirk, he stops, and picks up something from the bed. I watch as he tears open and rolls on a condom.

I inch further down the bed, closer to him. I gasp when he settles himself right where he's meant to be. His eyes hold mine as he slowly enters me, every last inch of him. I watch as his eyes darken and I see the struggle he's facing to keep them open. He's not the only one, but I'm hypnotised by the sight before me.

My muscles clench around him in anticipation, but also wanting to hold him there. He stays exactly where he is, not moving, just feeling. I can't wait any longer. I wrap my legs around his waist, showing him what I want.

That's all it takes. He pulls back and thrusts into me, going deeper than before. Shock waves ripple through my body at the intrusion. His hands grip tighter on my legs as he drives in and out.

My pulse pounds.

Each draw back and thrust sends my body soaring towards the final destination. My senses are overwhelmed. My muscles tense around him. I watch as his shoulders stiffen and I know he's as close to the finish line as I am.

I cry out as the fire within me explodes. Connor carries on thrusting harder, taking my body past the brink until he finds his own release.

He pulls me back up the bed with him until we reach the pillows. With both of us panting, he rolls me onto my side until I come face-to face with him. "I should tell you, we will be doing that again, because now that I've finally had you, once won't be nearly enough."

He kisses me on the nose and I close my eyes, hoping and praying the words he said are true. Once won't be enough for me either.

Chapter 12

HE'S NOT BESIDE ME. I don't even need to open my eyes to know that. His arms aren't wrapped tightly around my waist. Just the same as I don't need to open them to know that it's Tuesday morning. It's bright and sunny. I can already feel the heat coming through the open window. It's going to be a warm day. He kissed me before he left over an hour ago. I think I remember him telling me he was going for a run with Callum.

I've lay here since he left with a million things going around in my head. And the one thing I keep coming back to is; what the hell have I done? I've ruined the friendship we shared. This is a disaster.

Yesterday, I took the lead, which is so not me. It was what I wanted, but now I'm not so sure. The dynamics of our relationship has changed and there's a part of me that's scared I'll lose my friend.

I also found out Connor is a man of his word, not that there was ever any doubt, but when he told me last night we would be having sex again, part of me didn't believe him. We did and we even had a break when he phoned for a takeaway after he insisted we needed to eat. And the surprising thing was, I had actually worked up an appetite and I managed to eat everything on my plate. Connor joked that we would need to have sex a lot more if it meant I ate a full meal.

I couldn't bring myself to agree with him, even though a part of me did. Because sex with Connor was everything I could want and more.

Connor was attentive and playful all through the night. But now I know I need to leave his bed, come back to reality, and deal with whatever today brings. I checked my phone last night while we were having dinner. Callum had texted to tell me my interview was going to be aired in the States on the showbiz news at ten p.m. eastern. I'm now expecting Donovan to come back at me with something, although I'm unsure what. I'm dreading what he'll say. What lies he might tell, because even I know he won't tell the truth. There's no way a man who craves the attention of the showbiz lifestyle will take this lying down.

A door banging closed downstairs has me opening my eyes. I'm sure it's Connor, unless my Dad or Callum has decided to pay me a visit. I need to get up. I pull the covers off my naked body. Shit. Yesterday's clothes are lying in a heap on the floor. I have two choices: wrap a towel around me or put yesterday's clothes back on. I spot one of Connor's crisp white t-shirts folded neatly on the dresser.

Climbing out of bed, I walk toward the dresser and pull the t-shirt over my head. The bedroom door opens and in walks Connor, dripping in sweat after his morning run. And he still looks incredibly hot.

His dark eyes roam my body and stop at the hem of his t-shirt. "And here I thought you would be lying waiting on me so we could continue what we started."

"I'm sure we both have lots to deal with today."

"Ella . . . I'm sure we do," he says, strolling toward me. "But I'll always make time for you." I don't doubt the sincerity of his words; it's my own doubts that worry me. He places his hands on my shoulders. "Ella, stop thinking. Whatever is going through your head, push it to the side. Now, I think you should call Julie and go shopping with her today. You'll need a new dress for tomorrow night."

I sigh as I think of tomorrow night's red carpet event in the West End cinema. "I'm sure I've got something I can wear."

"I'm sure you have, but when I have you on my arm tomorrow night, I want to be sure you're feeling like yourself and are happy."

"I'm not sure about this." His soft eyes study me as I think about his words.

"Ella, you're overthinking again. Regardless of what I want to happen between us, I will always put your feelings before my own. You've already said you'll be there tomorrow night and I'd love nothing more than to have you on my arm and tell the world you're mine, but I won't. But, I'm also sure that you'll be in my arms, whether it's because you need my support or you just want to be close to me. So I think you should humour me and go shopping."

"Shopping! It was only a few days ago I couldn't even go shopping for basic food and now you want me to go and spend a small fortune on a dress."

He's still holding me but looking a bit bewildered. "Ella, I'm not saying spending a small fortune. I just want you to be happy when you walk down that red carpet tomorrow night."

"Sorry. I'm tired and stressed today." I'm unsure of what has just come over me and I know I should walk away from him, but I can't. He smiles and pulls my body to his, and I almost crumble.

"Come here. I take it now isn't a good time to tell you your phone has been ringing non-stop this morning?" he says, rubbing his hands up and down my back. I know this is wrong to want to be in his arms. The selfish part of me has no qualms about being here. But there's a part of me telling me not to lead him on.

It's too late for that.

"Has it?" I ask, sounding surprised, even though I should've expected it.

"Yeah, and Trevor wants you to call him. He wants to come over and speak to you about a few things."

"I see."

"And one of the news stations wants an exclusive interview with you and me."

"Why?" I lift my head and look into his eyes.

"Because of the pictures from Saturday night, both when we arrived and when we left."

Oh! I don't know about any from when we left, but I can only imagine how they looked considering my memory of the night is completely fuzzy. "Now, I need you to go and sort yourself before I remove my t-shirt from your sexy arse and I become a selfish git once again."

"I'm sorry." I break out of his hold and leave him alone in his bedroom.

"What the hell is wrong with me?" I ask myself when I'm finally back in my bedroom. I don't understand any of this. Connor is here and probably all the man any woman would need. He has everything going for him. The pull between us has grown rapidly in such a short space of time. Or has it always been there and it's only now that I'm noticing it? I don't know.

I'm so scared of my feelings. Scared of allowing myself to fall for someone else. Scared to have my heart broken in two again. What Connor and I want are two completely different things, I think. He hasn't denied his feelings for me, but I get the impression he wants a full relationship and I'm not sure about that. I don't want to be judged. But I do care a lot more than I had thought about him. Oh, God. I don't know what I want.

My life is so confusing.

I want to be happy. Maybe one day have a family. I want to fall in love with someone who loves me not for the fame or the money, but just for me. On the good days and the bad.

But with everything that's happened recently in my own life, I also want to help make a difference to others. I'm all too aware that if it weren't for my dad and the position he's in financially then things could be very different for me at the moment. The house, the cars would be repossessed and I'm not sure how I would cope ending up with nothing.

I'm fortunate. I've come from a privileged background in the sense that my parents had accomplished careers in the industry that I'm now a part of. But they tried to keep Callum and me grounded.

I'm lucky, but I know others aren't. What about those who find themselves losing everything they've worked so hard for. What happens to them when they lose not just possessions, but family and friends?

This is something that has been on my mind for weeks now. I'll speak to my dad and Trevor about this. I'm sure they'll be able to advise me further.

I pull off Connor's shirt and stand with it in my hands. It smells of him, and now of me. Us. This is so not good.

Maybe he should go and stay with Callum and give me some breathing space. Time to think about what I want because I'm not sure I can do that with him around.

Do you want to go shopping this afternoon? I text Julie.

Julie: Yes, just tell me where and when to meet you.

Me: Ok. I'm going for a shower and Trevor wants to come and see me.

Julie: Looking forward to seeing you and hearing all about Connor.

I have no idea how I'm going to manage avoiding the subject of Connor. Julie will want me to spill all the details about yesterday, but for me, some things should remain personal. But maybe with everything else going on, I should talk to her about how I'm feeling. She might help me to understand what's going on in my messed up head.

Or she might just get swept away on what I'm sure she'll see as a blossoming romance between two friends.

I need a shower. Hopefully it will help slow my mind down because I swear all these thoughts are going to send me mad.

"SO, THERE YOU have it," Trevor says as he finishes telling me all about the soap opera and the contract as we sit in my kitchen with papers spread all over the island. "I've had my lawyer and yours looking at this and they agree everything is in your favour. Now, I don't know much about the initial storyline you would be involved in, but that's something we would find out when we sit around the table with the producers."

"When can you set up a meeting?"

"They're keen to meet with you and Connor as soon as possible, so I reckon before the end of the week. I've also been sent a script for a major movie; a book adaptation that sounds interesting. I've still to read through the small print on that one, but as soon as I do, I'll send it over."

"Okay. Anything else?" I'm still waiting for him to mention Donovan's name and the reaction to my interview. I've been too scared to look online and see what is being said.

"Yes. Your interview is going down well. The response has been remarkable. You are being praised for speaking out in an industry where things like this happen on a daily basis, but no one wants to speak out because of fear of not progressing. That is a sad fact. I've seen it myself over the years when young actors have been taken advantage of. I know you're still feeling reluctant about what's going on but I think you've made the right decision in pressing charges against him. Do I think you'll get anything back? No, and Archie knows this too, but it might just help someone else in the long run."

"I know. That's the only reason I'm going through with it, because I just feel stupid."

"Enough, Ella. We've been through this. The young, mouthy girl I knew as she grew up and who I love wouldn't stand back in this situation. She would want to take back control."

"Trevor, I'm scared that girl is no longer here. That she's gone forever."

He comes around the table, sits beside me, and takes my hand. "Ella, you might be your father's daughter, but Betty and I love you just the same. We were never blessed with our own children but you and Callum are family to us. Always have been and always will be. The strong determined woman—because that's what you are—she's still there. Within reach. She's just biding her time, waiting for the right moment. I have no doubt she'll make her appearance soon enough. Something or *someone* will light the spark to bring our Ella back."

I throw my arms around him as my tears build and slowly fall.

"Ssh, come on. I don't want you crying." He rubs my back and I can't help hoping that he's right. The real Ella McGregor has been lost, and now I have to slowly find myself again. Footsteps entering the kitchen startle me. I lift my head to see Connor watching me with sadness on his perfect face.

So many unspoken words and feelings pass between us. But I do know that in order to find myself, I need to try and put whatever I'm feeling for Connor on the back burner and I think as he looks into my eyes, he already knows this.

I don't want to hurt him.

Chapter 13

"CAN YOU TELL ME WHY you've taken public transport?" Julie whines the question at me as I walk through the barrier at the train station. *And some say I'm a snob.*

"Hi to you too."

"Don't *hi* me. Why are we not meeting in some boutique to find you the perfect dress for tomorrow night?"

"Because I don't want to."

"So instead we're going shopping in the high street?"

This should make for an interesting afternoon.

"Yes, and the best bit is, I can guarantee no one will be wearing a dress from the high street tomorrow night."

"That's for sure." I can hear the sarcasm in her voice, but I choose to ignore it. Julie is very much high street for every day wear, but for special occasions, it has to be designer and exclusive. I suppose I've been the same. When money is no object, you don't think about it. But when it's gone, you have to make choices wisely. And having nothing the past few weeks has certainly given me a lot to think about.

We exit the station and Julie doesn't say another word as we head through the lane that will bring us out into one of the main shopping areas in Glasgow. The area is busy, people all in a hurry, rushing around. I notice a man sitting in the doorway; he might be a little older than me. He looks like he's not washed in God knows how long; could really do with a haircut and a shave. I pause as he asks passers-by for some spare change but everyone ignores him.

I walk towards him.

"Ella, what are you doing?" Julie asks, already looking as if she's about to freak out as I reach into my bag for my purse. "You do know he'll probably only use whatever you give him for alcohol or drugs?"

I ignore her because I can. I take a ten pound note from my purse and hand it to the man. He looks at me and the note. "Are you sure?" he asks. I nod. The man's face lights up and he quickly stands to his feet. "Thank you. Thank you." The words leave him in a rush and he gives me the briefest of hugs. I can hear Julie moan that I'll smell just as bad as him.

Yes, he smells, but not of alcohol. I think Julie has him all wrong.

He picks up his rucksack and jacket. "Thank you so much," he calls over his shoulder as he walks away. I watch him as he walks straight into a sandwich shop.

"So, drink and drugs was it?"

"What?"

"That poor man just wanted something to eat."

"So, we're now on a mission to help every homeless person you meet on the streets today?"

"No, but I've made his day. You'd have thought I'd just given him the most expensive gift in the world. Have you never wondered why he or others became homeless in the first place? What happened that was so bad in their lives? No? Well, lucky you. My thoughts these past few weeks have been so messed up that before I never really gave it much consideration. But when I thought I was going to lose everything . . ."

"You would never have lost everything because you have good

friends and family."

"You're right, but what about those people living on the street? What do they have? Nothing."

We're still standing in the street when the man comes out of the shop with a hot cup of tea or coffee and a hot filled roll. He smiles, passing me, taking a bite, and returns to where he was.

"Come on. Let's go and do this," Julie says, taking my hand and pulling me towards the high street. She really doesn't seem in the mood.

We flit from one shop to another, and I'll be honest, I find absolutely nothing suitable for a movie premiere. "Do you give in yet?" she asks as we leave yet another shop.

"No. We'll find something. I'm sure we will."

The next shop is called Inspire and, taking a deep breath, we enter. The first thing that hits me is the array of colours; everything from the latest in trend to plain, boring black. Already, I love the feel of this shop. The other thing I notice is that, unlike any of the other shops we've been in, the staff seem focused on customer service. There's a few members on the shop floor offering advice to some customers.

I turn and smile at Julie. "We're going to find something in here."

"We'll see. I think you'll be calling one of the boutiques to see if they have anything suitable," she says, walking off and pretending to look at some clothes on the rails. I wander around and I really love everything I see.

"Can I help you? You're Ella McGregor, aren't you?" a young sales assistant asks. She's almost bouncing on the spot.

"Yes, I am. And yes, I could do with some help."

"It would be my pleasure, Miss McGregor."

"Ella is fine. Now, I need you to point me in the direction of your dresses."

"Of course. Follow me." Julie shakes her head at me but

decides to follow us. "Is there something in particular you're interested in?"

"Yes. Something I can wear tomorrow night to a film premiere."

"You won't get anything in here," Julie says, loud enough to be heard. I might kill my best friend if she doesn't behave. What the hell has got into her today? She's never been this much of a bitch when we've been out before. There must be something wrong.

"I'm sure we will," I say with confidence. Julie huffs as she starts looking through the rails of dresses. I catch her smile as she takes a berry red dress from the rail. That's a first for today.

"Ella, is there any colour or style in particular you would like? We have a huge selection of maxi dresses and cocktail dresses. Give me a second and I'll ask the shop manager if there is any new stock I could let you see."

The sales assistant walks over to the tills and I watch as she excitedly tells her boss that I'm in the store. The other lady looks over a few times in almost disbelief at what the younger girl is saying.

"Ella, what do you think of this?" Julie asks, holding the berry red dress before her.

"With your skin tone, hair, and eye colouring that would be perfect on you. Why don't you go and try it on?"

"I think I will."

She disappears into the changing room and the assistant and shop manager walk over to me. The manager has a few dresses in her arms. "Miss McGregor, lovely to meet you. These dresses have only come into the shop this morning and, as yet, they haven't been put out on display. You're welcome to try them on."

"Thank you," I say as she and the assistant hold them up. My eyes instantly go to a beautiful black silver-embellished strapless maxi. "This one is stunning," I say, running my hands over the fabric.

"You have great taste," the manager says just as Julie steps out of the changing room. "Wow, it seems your friend has great taste too." Julie smiles and the manager walks toward her and has a good look all around the dress. "The berry dress is also a new style, but I think you should try it on in the smaller size. It's a little big around your back and hips."

She hands Julie a smaller size and my friend looks more than happy with what I think will be the dress she wears tomorrow night. "What size are you, Miss McGregor? An eight?"

"I'm usually a ten."

"Okay, but I think we can all agree you're not a ten. Go and try on the eight then we can take it from there. Now, am I right in thinking you want this for tomorrow night, if it's suitable?"

"Yes."

"Okay, go in and try it on. Once you're in the dress, one of us will come and do up the zip and clasp for you." The manager and assistant seem lovely. Yes, they are probably a bit more helpful because of who I am. They're both excited and I can't blame them for that.

Before I go into another changing room, Julie comes out wearing the size smaller and it's perfect on her.

"What do you think?" she asks, taking another look in the full size mirror.

"It's stunning. I love it," I say, turning to the manager and the assistant. They stand, nodding in agreement.

"I have shoes and a bag that would go with that. Give me a minute." I watch on as the young assistant leaves us briefly before returning with contrasting black and berry shoes and handbag. She's right; it all looks great together.

"Okay, I think I'm sorted for tomorrow. It's your turn." And here she was adamant that she wouldn't find anything suitable. I'm glad Julie got it wrong.

I take the black and silver dress and enter the changing room.

Removing my clothes and bra, I slip the dress on and shout for someone to fasten it up. The assistant comes in and her face lights up. I've avoided looking in the mirror because I have a feeling the look on Julie's face is what will seal the deal.

The assistant stands back and has a good look. "It's perfect. You look incredible. Let's go and show your friend."

I nod. "Bloody hell," says Julie as she throws her hand over her mouth. Her eyes roam every inch of the dress, taking all the detail in. "I really don't know what to say. You know I had my doubts about shopping for the perfect dress on the high street. Ladies, I'm sorry. I don't mean any offence," she says, turning to the manager and assistant. "But that dress on you is . . . it's so you. Everything about it, right down to the fishtail, which I wasn't sure would suit you. I love it."

Turning my head to the mirror, I finally allow myself to see it and, wow. Just wow. It has to be one of the most flattering dresses I've ever had on, and I've worn some amazing dresses. Julie's reaction was all I needed to see. It was priceless.

"I'll take it."

"What about shoes, bag, or even a shawl?" the young assistant asks.

"I'll trust your judgement." She rushes off and, within a few minutes, she's back with black shoes, a bag, and a shawl to match the dress. "I'll go and change," I say, heading back inside.

"A certain someone is going to love you in that dress," Julie calls after me, but I choose to ignore her, which is getting easier.

"Miss McGregor, thank you for shopping with us today. I hope you're happy with your purchases," the manager asks as we pay.

"Yes, but I do have a small favour to ask."

"Ask away."

"I'd appreciate it if this didn't end up in tomorrow morning's papers. Thursday's is fine."

"Of course, but we're not in the habit of blabbing to the press about our customers."

"I appreciate that, but if you want to use it for publicity you can after tomorrow night."

"That's very kind of you, Miss McGregor. I'll pass the message on to the owner."

Julie and I leave the shop happy and excited about our purchases. I know for a fact no one will have these on tomorrow night. Anyone who is or thinks they're someone special will have gone for an exclusive design.

We're chatting away as we walk back toward the train station. "You seemed out of sorts earlier," I say. "You were very judgemental."

"Sorry. I'm just not myself but I can't place what's wrong." I accept her answer. I'm sure when she's worked it out, she'll fill me in.

The homeless man I gave money to earlier is still there but there's now a crowd of young boys tormenting and teasing him.

This is wrong on so many levels.

I stop. "Ella, there's nothing more you can do," Julie says as I take in the situation. There's lots of people standing back, tutting as they look on at the situation, but no-one doing anything about the lads. In my book that is wrong. The people watching are no better than the lads.

"Maybe there is." She frowns and watches me as I take my phone from my bag and start searching the internet. I smile when I find what I'm looking for.

"You have gone insane," Julie says, peering over my shoulder, watching what I'm doing. "What the hell has happened to you?"

I shrug and walk through the crowd with my head dipped, hoping no one takes much notice of me. I move in front of the lads doing all the shouting and a couple of men in the crowd step forward to move them on.

About bloody time.

Bending down, the man lifts his head and looks at me. "Oh, hello."

"Hi. Sorry about the boys."

"Unless they belong to you, which I doubt, you're much too young, then you have nothing to be sorry for. Thank you for earlier."

"You're very welcome." I take a pen from my bag and scribble down the numbers he needs. "It's not much but it's the least I can do for you. Here are the details for a bed for tonight. It's not fancy, just a basic room in a hotel, but you'll have hot and cold water and a meal tonight and tomorrow."

"I can't accept this," he says, tears filling in his eyes.

"You can and you will. I won't take no for an answer."

"Really?" I nod. "You've no idea what this means to me. This means I can turn up for an interview clean and fresh tomorrow instead of looking like this. It means I stand a chance of putting what's left of my life back together."

"Glad to hear it."

We stand and I can hear Julie gasp. When I turn, her eyes are filled with tears. "Thank you so much. I have no way to repay your kindness."

"It's not needed. I hope and pray that you can get your life back together."

He nods, picking up his belongings, and walks away. He turns his head and waves over his shoulder. I turn and take Julie's hand and walk back through the crowd of people and I think I've gone completely un-noticed.

"Ella McGregor, what you've done and his reaction is totally priceless. You, my friend, are one of the kindest people I know."

"And you are a bit emotional."

"It must be near that time of the month for me."

Sometimes I think I am kind, but other times I just think I'm a lost soul, much like the man I just helped.

Chapter 14

"WHAT TIME ARE WE LEAVING?" Julie asks as we finish getting ready in the master bedroom. I didn't want to be in here but, according to Julie, the bedroom at the back of the house wasn't big enough for both of us and everything she's brought with her. She's even brought her make-up on wheels tonight. Bloody hell; she's too organised. Any normal person would've brought a make-up bag with a few essentials, but not Julie.

It's been really fun getting ready tonight. Julie has done my hair and make-up and I hardly recognise the person in the mirror. I know I was dressed up on Saturday for our night out but this is different. I'm sure many will class this as my first public appearance in months. I suppose, in a way, it is.

"Dad will be here in twenty minutes with Callum and we're all travelling together."

"Connor too?"

"Yes, Connor too." She smiles and stares but doesn't utter a word. I've told her this conversation is off limits at the moment until I find myself in a happier place. And I'm getting there. Slowly but surely. Connor has given me space since yesterday morning and, for that, I'm grateful. It's hard to think when he's around and, the strange thing is, when he isn't around, he's all I seem to think about.

It makes no sense. Or maybe it does.

Julie stands in her dress looking incredible; her hair, make-up, everything about her. She loves nights like these, probably more than me at times. "Right, lady. Time for you to get in that dress. I'll zip you into it but I know someone else will be desperate to zip you out of it."

"Julie, you're impossible," I screech, pulling the dress on. She smiles as she pulls the zip up. "Please don't make this any harder for me than it is tonight."

She stands behind me, leaning over my shoulder, and we're both looking into the mirror. "Ella, my gorgeous friend. Take a good look at you and tell me what you see."

I think about her words for a moment. "I see a woman who has been hurt. She's scared. But I also see the woman or girl I once was. I see her strength and determination. I see her kindness and her love. Little parts of me are returning."

"Okay, that's what you see. I see a woman who is strong-willed. Who is determined to push her life forward and stop living in the past. I see the love you have for your friends and family shine from you on a daily basis, even when we all drive you insane." She laughs a little. "But I see this gorgeous talented woman who has carved out an amazing career for herself. I feel lucky that she's my best friend in the whole world. But I also see her conflicted emotions that she has for a certain male friend, and, yes, I know this conversation is off limits. But I also see how he feels about you."

"Julie, please," I say, not knowing if my emotions can take any more.

"Okay, I'll stop, only because we don't have time for me to touch up your make-up. Now, tonight is all about looking glamorous and turning heads in our high street dresses."

"Come on. Let's get downstairs, so we're ready to leave as soon as the car gets here."

I slip the shoes on my feet and she hands me the bag and shawl and we leave the bedroom. Connor is downstairs; I can hear him moving around. I don't even know what he's wearing tonight. He's spent a lot of time with Callum and my dad since yesterday which has meant I've had the space I wanted, or rather, thought I wanted.

Crazy as it sounds, I've missed him.

Suddenly, there's knots in my stomach as I descend the stairs. This is ridiculous. When I reach the bottom, I stop, close my eyes, and gather my thoughts.

"Wow. Oh. My. God. You, Connor Andrews, are a sight for sore eyes," I hear Julie say as she enters my front room. I suppose I should go and see what all the fuss is about.

"You don't look so bad you . . ." Connor stops talking in the middle of his sentence when I enter the room. He stands by the large bay windows, surprised, his eyes glistening as he looks me over. "Ella, you look stunning." He takes slow steps toward me and suddenly it feels like it's only the two of us in the room. Our eyes meet and I feel a current of electricity run through my body. Julie is right; he is a sight for sore eyes in his family tartan. I should've expected him to wear it; after all, he's home in Scotland and this is a big event. I'm sure Callum and my dad will be wearing kilts.

I've seen him in a kilt before, but I've never taken the time to really appreciate how good he looks in it. Incredibly handsome. Everything from his well-groomed hair all the way down to his well-shined shoes. He oozes self-confidence, and why shouldn't he? This is why women fall at his feet.

"It's good to see you still wear the kilt well."

"I wear a lot of things well, as you know."

Julie coughs, clearing her throat, and I feel my face redden at what he's implying. Or maybe he's not implying anything and it's me that's got the wrong end of the stick.

He's now in touching distance and that's all I want to do;

touch him. Run my fingers along the roughness of the stubble along his jawline. I take a breath in and all I smell is the tantalizing smell of his aftershave.

"Okay, enough already, you two," Julie snaps, bringing me out of my Connor-induced state. "Any more of that and you, Connor Andrews, will be missing your own premiere. Now, I believe there is a car outside waiting on us."

"Okay," I say, reluctant to leave.

"Ella, before we go, I have to say it again and maybe you'll believe it. You look stunning; picture perfect. That dress, it was made for you. Where did you go shopping?"

"You really want to know?" He nods enthusiastically. "Inspire."

"You mean the high street chain?"

"Yes.

"Ella, by wearing that tonight you have probably single-handedly quadrupled their sales."

"Oh, Ella is all about helping others out," Julie pipes up. "Now, hurry up." Connor glances between us and I can already hear the unspoken question, but at this moment in time, I have no intention of telling him about yesterday. That can wait.

We follow Julie and I set the alarm before locking the door. "I told the manager she was free to advertise that I'm wearing one of their dresses after tonight."

"You're full of surprises," he says, taking my arm as we walk down the stairs. My brother and Dad are standing outside beside the black limousine that's parked in my driveway. They're both wearing kilts. They look incredibly handsome. I'm really lucky having them in my life. They're such a huge part of it.

"There she is, back where she belongs," my dad says, his eyes bursting with pride and filled with unshed tears.

"Don't you dare. You'll set me off and Julie says I can't ruin the make-up."

"Julie has a point. Sweetheart, you look like you again.

Something has put the sparkle back in my girl's eyes. Your mum would be so proud to see you looking so strong."

"For tonight, I am strong. I can't guarantee what I'll be like tomorrow but, hey, I'm giving it a go."

"You are and that's all I ask of you. I'm so proud of you and Callum. Now, let's get this man to his premiere on time."

I smile and greet my brother with a hug before climbing in.

"NOW, LADIES, REMEMBER there is a long walk to the entrance," my dad reminds us. It should only take five minutes at most from exiting the car to standing on the front steps. It's a pity the street the cinema is on is a pedestrian only zone. No cars are allowed. I'm sure there will be a red carpet laid for the entire walk down the street. And five minutes is a long walk.

The car stops and I'm not sure I'm ready for this. All cameras will be on Connor tonight and that means they'll be on the rest of our party too. Dad gets out, followed by Callum and then Julie. "Ella, are you ready?" We haven't spoken about tonight, and what it will mean for us being on his arm. I'm nervous but I hear the anticipation in his voice.

"Yes. I'm ready." I know what this will signal to the world of showbiz, but I'm more concerned about what it means for us. For our friendship. A friendship that, because I crossed a line, could hang in the balance.

He climbs out and there's cheering and cameras flashing, but Connor doesn't acknowledge anyone. He stands patiently waiting on me with his hand out. I finally give it to him and he helps me out of the car. Whistling, shouting, cameras flashing. This is the part I was dreading the most.

"Connor, a picture of you and your good lady," a photographer yells out.

"Shall we?"

I smile and nod, even though I feel tension running through my veins. His eyes fill with happiness as his smile fills his face. He wraps his arm around my waist and I lean my head on his shoulder as one photographer snaps away.

Another car pulls up, it's Trevor and Betty. I forgot they would be here. I hope I get a chance to catch up with her after the showing, but if not, I'm going to make the time this week to go and see the woman I've always seen as my other mum.

They greet us before walking a little further on with my dad. Callum is posing with Julie and they look good together, but I don't think they'll ever be anything more than friends. But then again, I thought that about Connor.

And, in my head, we are certainly more than friends, and this is where it gets complicated for me.

"Are either of you going to confirm that you're now seeing each other?" The question is called out from a reporter.

"Oh, come on. This isn't the time to confirm or deny your allegations. But Miss McGregor is my friend. Always has been and always will be."

"So, you are both still very much single and on the market?"

I look him in the eyes and something clicks, "Oh, I don't know about that," I say, not to the reporter but to Connor, bringing the biggest grin to his face. There's a tingling in my stomach as he leans forward and dips his head, claiming my lips with his in the softest of kisses, sending shivers all through my body.

A few days and he's turned my life upside down. Or maybe he's just helped me see what he's seen all along which is . . . that we could be really good together.

"You and I need to talk," he whispers against my lips, breaking our kiss.

"Yes, I think we do, but tonight is your night to enjoy."

"The only thing I plan on enjoying is you. Is it too early to leave?" I laugh at him and he turns me away from the cameras and we walk to the entrance where the others are waiting. Julie has a stupid grin on her face. My dad has a look of concern but there's also a slight happiness lingering in his eyes as well.

Inside, it's really busy. Everyone who is anybody is here; a few big names from Hollywood, along with their partners. I've always loved the social aspect of nights like tonight. It will be good to catch up with a few acquaintances. We're each handed a glass of champagne. Connor keeps my hand in his as various people come over and speak to us. Dad is standing with Julie, Trevor, and Betty; all talking. My brother is standing with a couple of football players. I smile as I realise who he's with; Fletcher Adams and Logan Walker.

I might not be interested in football, but I do know who they are, because they're always making headline news. I swear they make the headlines more than I do. I see their wives standing at the side, both stunning women. Jessica Adams is probably a woman I should introduce myself to, because she might be able to help me work out what I want to do. After all, she's now doing lots of work at highlighting domestic violence. I'll speak to Callum and he can introduce me to her and Fletcher.

"I didn't think I would be seeing you again so soon." I turn and I'm facing Alex Mathews and his wife Libby. "Libby, this is Ella, and the man of the night, Connor Andrews."

"A pleasure to meet you both," Libby says.

"And you," I say as I take a look at them together. It's funny seeing Alex standing here with his arm around his wife's waist, looking so happy and relaxed. He never looked like this in Katherine Hunter's company. There was never a sparkle in his eye; not like now.

"Alex told me you were at the club on Saturday and mentioned maybe meeting up and having some lunch," she says as Connor and Alex talk about the movie.

"It would be great if you have the time. I know how busy you must be with the hotel and your children."

"They all keep me on my toes, but getting an hour or so to myself to catch up with adults is also important and I know Alex would love to catch up with you."

"Well, he has my number now so when you're free, just give me a call."

"Mum, Dad, you made it." I turn back to Connor's voice in time to see his parents walking toward us.

"We'll leave you to it," Libby says, giving me a kiss on the cheek.

"Speak to you both later on," I say to Libby and Alex.

"Of course we made it. Did you really think we would miss our boy's premiere here in his home country?" She kisses Connor and he looks totally made up that his parents made it. "Ella, you look beautiful, as always." His mum takes me in her arms and gives me a hug.

"Thank you. It's great to see you both again."

"We're so excited. You know this is the first time we've been to a premiere," his dad tells me.

They are both bursting with pride as they talk, and why shouldn't they be? Connor is one of the hardest working actors I know, and with hard work comes success. They should enjoy tonight.

An announcement is made for everyone to enter the screening room. Everyone starts to head inside. The rest of our party comes over and wishes Connor good luck. My dad takes his parents with him. I turn to give Connor a brief kiss.

"You are staying right by my side the whole night," Connor tells me, taking my hand in his. He leads me through the crowd and all the way down to where the rest of the cast and directors are sitting.

Silence descends around the room as the screen comes to life.

Chapter 15

"I WAS BEGINNING TO THINK Connor wasn't going to let you go." Julie giggles, handing me another drink. I look around the room and it's packed; everyone is excitedly talking about the movie. It's had a great response and I'm sure it will break box office sales.

"I have no idea what you're talking about," I say smugly. She's right; he reluctantly let me go when I excused myself to go to the ladies.

"Yeah, right. He's desperate to get you all to himself."

I have no reply to that because I can't wait until we can leave, but he can't leave his own after party early. I stand with Julie, my dad, and Trevor and Betty, and watch, smiling, as Connor works his way around the room. Connor's parents left about twenty minutes ago. They couldn't hide how proud they were of him, but his mum was tired. I got a chance to catch up with Betty and I've promised to go and visit her this week. She told me I'd better go so she can feed me, and that I should bring my new hunk of a man.

Connor's parents loved being here; the film is amazing and Connor was perfect for the leading role as detective Chris Stone. His Mum has tried to encourage him to go and stay with them for a few days. He said he would wait and see what was happening in the next few weeks. As he spoke to her, her eyes darted between me and her son and I'm sure she realised I was the reason he wanted to stay here in Glasgow.

Connor has a bottle of beer in his hand, but I've not seen him take a drink from it in the last ten minutes. He might be mingling, but his eyes have been on me most of the time, burning with a deep intensity across the room.

"So, what now? That was one hell of a kiss and I'm sure it's already viral and on every social media site in the world," Julie says. She has a point and I can't make up my mind if that's a good or a bad thing. For once it would be nice to have some sort of privacy, but I know I'll never get it.

"I don't know. I guess Connor and I talk." We should do that before we do anything else.

"Is that before or after he undresses you tonight?"

"Julie!"

"I'm keeping it real."

Callum approaches us with Fletcher and Jessica Adams. I had mentioned to him that I wanted to meet them; my brother seemed a little surprised, but said he would sort it. "Ella, Julie, this is Fletch and Jess."

"Hi," we say in unison. "Actually, Jess, you might be able to help me. Offer me some advice."

"If I can."

Everyone looks at me and I can already tell Callum and Julie are curious to hear what I have to say.

"I know you're now doing a lot of charity work for Women's Aid and I'm looking for some advice. I won't go into all the details now, but I'm really interested in trying to raise money for homeless people."

"Wow!" Julie and my brother say. Callum seems more shocked than my friend, but then again, Julie was with me yesterday.

"Really?" Callum asks.

"Yes, really."

"Why don't we meet up this week?" Jess says. "It would have to be at night and at mine because of the baby, but I'm more than happy to offer you advice if I can."

"Thank you. I appreciate it."

"I also think there may be someone else in this room that might consider helping you, sis," Callum says, turning around and staring across the room. "Alex, can we have a word?" I hadn't thought about Alex. He and Libby walk toward our growing party.

"What can I do for you?" Alex asks.

"I'm not sure if it's something you might be interested in, but Ella would like to do some charitable work. I heard through the grapevine you were interested in doing some more for charity."

"You heard correct, I've just not done anything about it yet. I'm sure we can talk." This all sounds really interesting; Alex Mathews and Jessica Adams. I'm sure they can offer me the help and advice I need.

"I don't know what to say, but thank you. Both of you."

"Who are you thanking?" Connor asks, slipping his arm around my waist and bringing a huge smile to my face.

"Jess and Alex. I've been thinking something over and they've offered to help me if they can."

"Sounds good." Callum launches into a brief rundown of what I've mentioned. Alex and Fletcher talk football while us ladies talk about how good the night has been. It appears the two have met once or twice before.

Conversation flows with ease, leaving me feeling contented and fortunate. Libby and Jess seem really friendly and outgoing. "Ella, I know you're in the middle of a conversation, but I really, really want us to leave. Now. Together," Connor whispers against my neck, placing a kiss just under my ear, sending a shockwave of desire through my body.

"Is there anyone else you need to see?" I ask.

"No. How quickly can we leave?"

Jess laughs and I realise everyone is looking at us. "I think you two should go," she says, smiling. Fletcher has his arm around her shoulder and everyone's eyes are on us. We say goodbye to everyone, and Julie tells me she wants all the juicy details tomorrow at dinner.

With Connor's hand in mine, we leave. Stepping outside into the cold night air, I had completely forgotten there would still be a few photographers hanging around. The flashing startles me, but Connor pulls me closer to him. He called a taxi and it's waiting where we were dropped off. We pose for a couple of pictures before making the walk along the street.

"Here we are," Connor says, opening the taxi door. He gives the driver my address and takes the seat beside me. "Are you okay about earlier?"

"Yes. Connor, I have feelings that are scaring me and I can tell from the smile on your face that my little admission pleases you. But I really do value the friendship we have."

"Of course I'm happy. And you don't have to be scared. I will never hurt you or abandon you. I will certainly never take you for granted. And someone very dear to me once told me the greatest foundation for a relationship is friendship. We have that so we can build on it." He presses a soft kiss to my lips. I hope he's right.

I CLOSE THE door behind us and lock it. Neither of us is going anywhere else tonight. I slip my shoes off.

"Are we going to talk or are you allowing me to take you upstairs and worship your body?"

I step into Connor's arms, running my fingers along his jawline. "Take me to bed," I whisper.

He doesn't need to be told twice. "I'm taking you to bed, but don't expect to get any sleep. I'm going to have you screaming my name over and over," he says, scooping me up in his arms, and I can't help but yelp as he does. I wrap my arms around his neck, holding him tight, and watch him. All I want to do is kiss him. I've longed to have his lips on mine since he kissed me on the red carpet.

Julie is right; that kiss will have gone viral. It will be there for the world to see. The funny thing is, I don't care who sees it.

He pushes open his bedroom door with his foot and strides toward the bed. All I can do is smile in his arms. This already seems familiar and so normal. I close my eyes, absorbing all comfort from our closeness. Everything with Connor is relaxed and easy.

He stops and I open my eyes and jump from his arms. We really have been here before, but tonight isn't about taking what I want. It's about me giving myself to him freely.

"Now, if this was a date I would've brought you home and got to kiss you goodnight on the front doorstep."

"Yes, but would you have settled for just a goodnight kiss?" My breath is already sounding raspy.

He takes one slow step toward me. I shiver from the proximity. "No. I think we would've stepped inside and I would have grabbed your body tight, pushing you against the door." He grabs me and I throw my arms around his neck. "You would've thrown your arms around my neck, and I'd pull your body closer to mine." He pulls my arse tight to him. "And you would giggle before wrapping your legs around my waist, your dress riding up and bunching around your waist. Then I'd have my way with you in the hallway."

With his eyes on mine, he runs a hand up my back. "But, that's not what you deserve tonight. I'm sure there'll be other days for a hard and fast fuck against the door." I gasp at his words. "Tonight you are mine to enjoy and devour. But first I need to get out of this damn kilt."

"I'm more than happy to help with that," I say, raising my

hands and slowly removing his jacket.

Once the jacket is off, he takes my face in his hands, his grip tight. He very slowly lowers his face to mine. That delicious mouth of his brushes gently against mine. I want him to do so much more with his mouth. Desperation races through my body and I'm certain Connor can feel my need as much as I can. But if he does, he's not in any rush to do anything about it. This kiss is tender. I have a deep urge to alter the pace, but Connor's in control.

It takes a few minutes before my lips accept their fate and give in to the gentle taste of him. He lifts my legs tightly, my dress riding high as he said it would only moments ago. With our lips locked, enjoying each other, his erotic words from moments ago flood my mind; that is exactly what I want right now. My body fits perfectly against his. His erection fits between my legs and all I want is to tear his kilt from his waist.

Desire can be felt in the air around us, reaching dizzying heights, and still he continues with the slow and precise torturous pace. My fingers pull gently on his hair as I run them through it, pleading with him for more.

He pulls back, casts his eyes over my now swollen lips, before smiling and looking me in the eye. "If this was a date I would be saying goodnight."

"But it's not and you're staying here with me."

"No, it's not. But I sense what you really want," he says as he starts walking with my legs still wrapped around his waist toward the bathroom. "You want rough and I want sweet and loving. So we should compromise. I'll give you what you want if I can take what I want."

How can I argue with that? For me that's a win-win.

He pushes open the bathroom door and finally puts me back down on my feet. I'm dizzy from our intoxicating kiss. A kiss that has left me breathless and has turned my knees to jelly.

A kiss, that's all it was. And here I am as giddy as a school girl.

"Can you unzip me," I ask, already turning my back to him. It takes him a moment. I don't know what he's thinking about before I feel his fingers on my dress and he slowly lowers my zip and my dress falls to the floor. I step out of it.

Turning back around to face him, I'm wearing only black lace knickers. I really need more clothes that call for a bra. There's not a lot left for him to remove. I watch as he starts undressing and, bloody hell, there's so much clothing to remove.

Finally, he gets to the kilt and I watch with baited breath because I'm a little curious to find out if, tonight, he is, in fact, a true Scotsman. With his hand on the last fastening, he stares, a wicked smirk on his face. "Is this what is so interesting?" he asks as the kilt falls to the floor at his feet.

I nod in appreciation at the sight before me. As if there was ever any doubt in my mind that Connor Andrews would be a true Scotsman. "All that's standing in our way now is those sexy lace knickers."

"Is that so?" I say, grabbing the waistband of them. I bend and lower them down my legs until I step out of them. "Well, they're not in the way now."

"No, they're not." I reach out and smooth a hand over his chest. He smiles and pulls my body tight against him, pressing a hard kiss to my lips. My body tenses momentarily against his before he starts walking, still with his lips on mine and arms wrapped around me. "Foot up and step back, and now the other," he says, breathless against me.

I do as he tells me. His lips leave mine and I close my eyes and wait. The sound and feel of the rushing water has me opening my eyes. I bring my hand up and wipe away some water from my eyes so I can see him. Briefly, I see the fire in his eyes before his lips find mine again.

With warm water cascading around us, I'm drowning in the

intensity of our shared kiss. His fingers trace lightly over my back as my own fingernails dig into his shoulders, trying to coax him into speeding things up between us.

I slide my hand down between us, taking hold of his erection. I pause for a moment, before sliding my hand up and down. He groans against me. I line him up and adjust my body so that he slides against me as I move my hips. And it's right there, pressing against me in the exact place I need it to be. My breath hitches and my fingernails dig in deeper.

"I need to have you," he says against my neck as he presses kisses against it. I'm speechless. "Turn around and press your hands on the wall." I do as he says and I gasp as he pulls my hips to him.

He doesn't give me any warning before driving deep and hard into me. My body burns with desire. This is what I wanted. This is what I needed. Hard and fast.

I close my eyes and allow my feelings to take over. I'm lost, totally lost to him moving in and out, each time going that little bit deeper. Claiming another part of me as his. I push back against him, wanting to feel more.

I open my eyes and look down at where we're joined and watch as he drives in and out. The sight of him sliding in and out is pushing me close to the edge. Removing one hand from the wall, I reach down and feel him as he thrusts hard against me. My one small act causes him to react; a rough growl vibrates against me as his wet lips dance across my back.

With the water falling, the pace quickens. My body tenses. My muscles tighten around him.

Desire consumes me and I can't concentrate

My breathing quickens until I'm crying out his name and he's pounding harder and harder until my name falls from his lips. He continues to rock against me.

Something clicks in this moment for me.

Words can't describe it, but there's something there.

With jelly legs and a thundering heartbeat, I turn back around, wrap my arms around his neck, and press my lips lightly against his. "That was round one. Don't think for a minute that is the only round of the night. Far from it. You are now mine for the rest of the night to worship and enjoy and I plan on doing both."

Chapter 16

"ELLA, YOU NEED TO GET up." It feels like a dream, but I sense his breath against me and hear the soft tone of his voice whisper against my skin. "Come on, sleepy head. You need to get up." Why isn't he still in bed beside me? He should be here with me. Neither of us have had much sleep, but it was so worth it.

"Why? Please let me sleep," I whine, refusing to open my eyes. I clench them tight, screwing my face up in the process. This must be so unattractive. "You kept me up all night so the least you can do is let me rest." My mind and body are exhausted. I'm going to sleep for at least twenty-four hours just to recover from our night time activities. He is certainly fitter than me.

"I'm sorry," he says, tugging the covers from my body. I try to keep them but he's strong. Fine, I'll just lie here naked, it won't bother me. "Ella, babe, I'm not kidding. You need to get up before your dad comes up the stairs."

That does it. I open my eyes and see the concern in his. Why would my dad be here at . . . I look at the time—ten a.m.—after last night? "Why is he here?"

"Trevor is here too. Go and grab a shower and get your sexy arse downstairs. If you're lucky, I'll even make you a cup of tea." He kisses the top of my head.

"Fine. You better throw in a chocolate biscuit or two as well,"

I huff with a playful smile on my face, sliding my legs off the side of the bed. I stomp across the bedroom to the bathroom, wiggling my arse as I walk. His loud inhale of breath makes me chuckle. I stop at the bathroom door and glance back over my shoulder. He smiles, shaking his head.

I close the door behind me and memories of last night fill my head. Shower sex is fun. Actually, sex with Connor Andrews is more than fun, it's incredible, and at the moment, that's all I want. Turning on the shower, I step under the water. I press my thighs together in an attempt to calm the urge there.

I shouldn't be thinking about sex when my dad and Trevor are downstairs waiting on me. I shake my head and lose all thoughts of Connor.

Hopefully, they won't be here for long. Although, I'm sure there is a very good reason they're here and I could bet on that reason being Donovan Bell. It's been all too quiet from L.A. I really expected him to come out fighting against me. I'm ready for the backlash. Yes, it's only been a few days since the first pictures of Connor and I went viral, but I still expected something, especially after my interview.

Maybe that's why they're here. Maybe Donovan has given his own interview.

I won't find out standing under the warm running water. I should get my arse in gear and down the stairs.

"WELL, DON'T YOU all look cosy," I say as I enter my kitchen. The three of them are sitting around the island, drinking tea, and there's a plate of chocolate biscuits in the middle, but no one is eating any. The thought that Connor has put them there for me makes me smile.

"Yes, well we should. We've had to wait long enough for you," Dad says as I sit down beside Connor. Connor places his hand on my knee and rubs it gently. The hairs on the back of my neck stand to attention and I'm suddenly worried.

"What's wrong?" I ask nervously, taking my mug of tea in both hands.

"Well . . ."

"Stop. Can you just tell her?" Connor says abruptly, causing my dad to frown.

Trevor leans forward. "Ella, there's a few things we need to discuss. Firstly, I've been sent a script and I've had a quick read over it and, all in all, it has the potential to be a huge blockbuster."

"What's the catch?"

"You're on the producer and director shortlist."

"Okay, this sounds interesting. Who else are they considering?" It's usual practice for a production team to have a few candidates for the leading roles.

"There's only you and Miss Hunter," Trevor tells me, shifting a little in the seat.

"Katherine Hunter!" The blonde actress that seems to cause trouble wherever she goes. The woman who also appears to be Donovan's new love interest. This is why the three of them are sat in my kitchen and I can see they're all wondering how this news will affect me.

"Yes."

"Okay." I can feel Connor's eyes on me. I don't turn to him because I don't want to see him feeling sorry for me. "So, what else is there?" I ask in an attempt to brush it off. Three sets of eyes watch me before they look at each other.

"Right, well, you and Julie have certainly made headlines up and down the country with your choice of dresses last night. I must say, you both looked gorgeous. But you are certainly causing a storm. The high street chain's social media is going crazy and so has my phone this morning."

"Sweetheart, Trevor has been taking phone calls since before five a.m. Several of the national papers want to run exclusive interviews with you, and the CEO of the high street chain has also been in contact to thank you and to ask if you would consider becoming the face of the company. He wants you to represent them."

"Wow, that's interesting."

"Ella," Trevor interrupts. "They want to meet with you as soon as possible."

"Okay, then arrange it. I don't have much else in my diary at the moment."

"I'll contact them soon and set up a meeting. We should also talk, while I have you both together, about that kiss." Connor and I exchange glances. We should've spoken about this. I have no idea what to say to my dad or Trevor about us.

"Guys, I'm sorry. I should've thought about the aftermath, but I don't regret doing it," Connor says, totally focused on me. "So, I'll apologise if this has caused more problems, but I won't apologise for showing my feelings."

My eyes drop to the table only for a moment, but long enough for Connor to notice. He takes hold of my hand and squeezes it tightly. Lifting my head, I meet his eyes and offer him half a smile. His feelings for me are there in front of me to see and it scares the hell out of me. He's not hiding his emotions well at all.

"Ella, Connor." It's Trevor's voice that has us looking across the island. "The question has been asked on more than one occasion so far this morning. I need to know how to answer it. Are you a couple?"

I look at my dad and he's waiting to hear the answer to this question. When I turn and look at Connor, he has the same look of anticipation on his face. He's waiting for me to answer this one. I take a deep breath. "Yes," I say, looking into Connor's eyes. His face lights up like a Christmas tree. God, he looks totally adorable right now.

"Connor," my dad's voice carries over to us. We turn and my dad smiles at me. "I have an idea of what Ella means to you, and to me, you are and have been part of our family for a number of years, but with what has happened in the past, I'm sure you'll understand my reservations for any new relationship she enters into."

"Dad!"

"Ella, your dad is right and we have so much to talk about," Connor tells me. I nod in agreement because I'm sure my answer has given him a lot to think about. I know it's given me lots to think about.

"Dad, Trevor, is there anything else?" I ask.

"If you mean has there been anything from Donovan, then no, there's nothing yet. But as soon as there's even the slightest whisper, you'll be the first to know," Trevor tells me, and relief sweeps over me.

But my relief is short lived as I realise I want Donovan to have something to say. The fact that he's been so silent is un-nerving. I've never known him to be this quiet. I know him well. Worry sweeps over me as I think about the fact he's most likely plotting against me. I know without a shadow of a doubt that he will have something up his sleeve. I'll need to be on my guard, as will Connor.

"Now, do you not have something you want to discuss?"

"Yes, although I'm not sure what organisation I should con-tact." Dad and Trevor look at each other, and I know they're both wondering what the hell I'm going to say next.

"The last few weeks I've had lots of time to think about what was going to happen to me if things didn't work out."

"Things would've worked out quicker if you hadn't decided to try and deal with everything on your own."

"Dad, I know that. But while I've been thinking, it's not been just about me."

"What do you mean?"

"Well, I'm fortunate, but what about those who aren't? If I had lost this house and the cars, what is the worst thing that would have happened to me? I'd have come and stayed with you or Callum until I got myself back on my feet. And with what I do for a living, let's face it, it really wouldn't take me long to get back in a better place. But what about those people who lose everything and find themselves with nowhere to turn?"

"Sweetheart, you are so like your mother. Always thinking of others." He might be right, especially when I think back to all the charitable causes she helped over the years.

"I want to do something for charity. The other day I gave a homeless man some money and he surprised Julie with actually going into a café and buying himself some food and a drink. He was maybe a little older than me. He was sleeping in a doorway and I know he wasn't the only one. When Julie and I finished shopping he was still there and a bunch of young lads were making fun of him. I ended up booking a room for him in one of the inns."

"Ella!"

"Don't. That man was so appreciative. He couldn't stop thanking me. It turns out he had a job interview yesterday and with staying at the inn, it meant he could shower, sleep, and turn up to the interview looking refreshed."

"So what do you want to do?" Trevor asks.

"I'm not entirely sure. I spoke to Jess and Fletcher Adams last night along with Mr and Mrs Mathews. I know the Adams' both work tirelessly highlighting domestic abuse. Jess has said she is more than happy to meet up with me."

"Okay, I'll look into it for you," Dad says with a warm smile. "I can tell this means a lot to you."

"It does."

He stands up. "Okay, sweetheart. We'll go and let you talk." I quickly go to him and wrap my arms around him. "Hey, what's this for?"

"Do I really need an excuse?"

"No, you don't, and you'll never get too old to give your old man a hug, I hope."

I walk with him out to the hallway and I can hear Trevor and Connor following behind us. Opening the front door, it's just Dad's car in my drive. "Trevor will call you later as soon as he has the meeting set up and I'll speak to you tomorrow. That should give you two time to talk. And I mean it. Talk and listen to him."

Dad gives me a kiss and walks towards the car with Trevor. I'm left standing in the doorway with Connor behind me. His arms wrap tightly around my back and his head rests against my shoulder.

"So, we have a few things to talk about. And you have a script to read over."

"Yes, it would appear so," I say, turning in his arms to face him. "But first I'd like a kiss, then another cup of tea so I can eat the chocolate biscuits." I throw my arms around his neck and stand on my tiptoes.

"You're very demanding," he says softly, his lips touching mine. "But because you've said you'll eat the biscuits, I'll let you have a kiss," he teases, a playful smirk on his handsome face. I close my eyes and allow my senses to take over. The taste and feel of his lips against mine all feels too comforting. The warmth of his body as I press against him feels natural. Everything so far with Connor feels natural. Maybe that's why I didn't hesitate when Trevor asked the question, even though I'm a bit concerned about changing the dynamics of our relationship.

With our lips lightly brushing the other's, I push my concerns away in the back of my mind where they can stay until I need to deal with them. And today isn't the time to deal with those. Or maybe it is.

I pull back and I'm greeted with a huge smile that reaches all the way to his dazzling eyes that are clouding over and filling with a deep desire. *Fuck. I want him.* "What are you so happy about?"

"Me? I have lots to be happy about. There's you. Us. But most importantly, you want to eat." His voice is low, full of longing and excitement. He takes my hand in his and I close the front door and allow him to lead the way back to the kitchen. He sits me down and leaves me watching him as he effortlessly moves around my kitchen, making a cup of tea.

I have the perfect view of him. Connor Andrews has a certain rough edge to how he looks today; this is the first time I've noticed it. I'm practically drooling over him with my elbows on the island and my hands propping up my face.

It feels good having someone do something for me. I know I must be grinning from ear to ear, but I can't help it and I don't want to hide how happy I'm feeling in this moment. Why should I?

With two cups in his hands, he walks back toward me, his eyes glistening. He sits opposite me and slides my tea over, along with a chocolate biscuit. Chocolate orange; one of my favourites. I slowly unwrap the biscuit and bite into it, savouring the taste. It's heavenly.

"Okay, if you keep that up, we won't be doing much talking. Can you not just eat the damn biscuit instead of making it sound so bloody erotic?"

Smiling, I shrug my shoulders. I have no words.

"With you making those noises, I don't want to talk. I have the urge to push everything out of the way and fuck you here and now."

Oh.

"Why don't you?" I'm pressing my legs together tightly under the table, trying to ease the pressure that has built up quickly.

"Because first we talk, then we'll m . . . fuck."

Chapter 17

I BLOT OUT HIS SLIP of the tongue, not wanting to think about his words. I know I should think about it. This between us feels right. There's no awkwardness, when I thought maybe there would be.

"Where will we start then?" I ask, taking another mouthful of the biscuit.

"Well, seeing as you're so preoccupied, I'll start." I would laugh if my mouth wasn't full of a chocolate orange biscuit. If I keep eating these, I won't be long in putting the weight I've lost and more back on. "Your word surprised me. Shocked me even."

"Me shock you? Now there's the surprise. Well, I wasn't going to lie, especially not to my dad, and Trevor will have a lot to deal with. I didn't see the point in making his job any harder because neither of us can be honest."

"So, we are going to give being a couple a go?"

"Yes. Connor, I can't explain it and I know it probably shouldn't feel right, but it does. I thought it would feel strange, because we've been friends for so long. I'm also a little scared that I'll lose you as a friend if . . ."

"Don't. I don't want it to ever feel strange or awkward. If it does, you have to tell me. Because, believe it or not, you mean the absolute world to me and I'm sure everyone else knew that fact a long time ago, including Donovan."

He pauses and I allow his words to sink in. Julie knew, Callum knew. What about my dad? Has he been aware of Connor's feelings for me too? I already know that answer; he said as much before he left. So it was only me that was left in the dark.

"Ella, what are you thinking?"

"That I've been blind with not seeing what was right in front of me."

"And what do you see?"

"A man who cares about me. A man who isn't scared to show his feelings. A man who has waited patiently for his chance while watching his best friend be a complete arse. Tell me, Connor, when did he first cheat on me?"

He closes his eyes. "About two years ago," he says quietly. He opens his eyes. "I'm sorry. I wanted to tell you but then it would've only looked like I had said it out of spite. For my own gain."

"Don't be sorry. This isn't on you and I don't blame you. The funny thing is, deep down, I already knew what you've confirmed. It's strange though, because up until about two years ago, there was lots of talk about us getting married, even though he never actually proposed. Could you imagine that? Ella Bell?" I laugh at how ridiculous that sounds, but stop when I see the hurt in his eyes.

He reaches his hands out to me and I give him mine. "Ella, I broke my own heart every day watching you with him. I've stuck around being his friend only because of you. Donovan and I should've parted company a long time ago. I want us to slow things down. I need us to have a fighting chance of survival because I'm not sure I'll be able to function not having you in my life. But I want more than friendship. I want you and a future together."

I'm not sure why, but his words take me by surprise.

"Why me?"

"Because you're it for me. You have been since that very first night. You took my breath away with your natural beauty and your perfect smile. You stole my heart that night. But, it's not just about that first night, I've watched you over the years. Watched how you've dealt with situations with your strength and determination. But, for me, I've had to watch on when Donovan has fucked up and all I've thought about is how he wasn't worthy of you, and how you ought to have someone who would treat you with the respect you deserve."

Wow!

"As I said we can slow this down between us."

"What happens if I don't want you to slow things down? I like the pace that has been set."

"Then we'll go at that pace and see where we end up."

"I'm hoping for the bedroom." I watch as he seductively licks his lips and I enjoy watching the amusement on his face.

"Ella!" He stands, and the chair scrapes along the floor. I take another biscuit and have a mouthful. He watches as I continue to munch away. "To me it looks like you're enjoying that biscuit way too much."

He has a point. Biscuit or sex? I know what my choice is.

My heart rate accelerates as he steps toward me with confidence. He's trying to keep a straight face but failing miserably. The corners of his mouth are twitching and any second now . . . Yes, there it is; his smile.

Leaning forward, he takes the biscuit from my hand and takes a bite. He makes chewing a damn biscuit look so seductive. *Bloody hell.* When he's finished eating, he takes another two steps until he's standing behind me.

I clasp my hands together.

"What do you want to do now?" he asks, draping his arms around me and nuzzling my neck. I close my eyes and enjoy the feel of him. He moves my hair and kisses my neck. My senses take over. The softness of his lips against my skin has it tingling all over.

Still kissing my neck, his hands move. He brushes against my breast, once, twice, before kneading it. My head rolls back. Desire spreads like wild fire through my body. All thoughts of my biscuits have melted away and been replaced by need.

I wanted the bedroom, but I'm not sure my body can wait that long. A small moan falls from my now parted lips. "Do you like this?" he asks, whispering against my ear.

"Yes, but I like you more."

"Ella, what do you want?"

"You." I turn in the chair and he steps to the side, holds out his hands, which I take, and he gently pulls me from the chair.

Chapter 18

EVERYTHING IS SO FAST PACED in showbiz. Why can't it just slow down for once? As I sit in the back of the car with Trevor, staring outside, watching people hurrying about getting on with their own business, I'm grateful for my time alone with Connor yesterday. Yes, my phone and his buzzed all day long, but it was only Trevor we replied to. For the next two weeks, we both have constant meetings about various projects.

It's all really exciting. And, for me, that's a huge bonus. I've not been excited about working for the past six months or so. Something was always missing. I couldn't tell you what it was, but I just had that feeling.

In a world where everything changes and happens so quickly, I'd love to slow the pace down. But as it is, I'm grateful for everything I have in my life at the moment. My family, my friends, and new beginnings.

The next chapter in my life starts today. Well, I suppose it started with Connor, but today I'm meeting with the CEO of the high street chain Inspire. He's coming from London especially to meet with me. Then we're going into his Glasgow store where I've to pick out items from the range to do a photoshoot for his company.

I declined the fee offered to me for the photoshoot. Instead,

I've asked that what I was going to be paid is put to charity. Trevor told me the company was more than happy to do that; they emailed him a contract last night with all the details on it.

Trevor and my dad worked hard on my behalf yesterday and this morning. After Connor and I spent some quality time together, he helped me decide what charity I wanted to help. Trevor has set up a meeting for next week and Connor has asked if he can come with me. He'd like to help out as well. I told him he didn't need to feel obligated to help because of me. But he assured me he wanted to help.

Actually, I think my dad wants to get in on the act as well. I think he's bored. Since Mum died, he's had a few acting jobs. He's been offered parts left and right, but turns most of them down. I'm not sure why; it would keep him occupied and give him something to do with all his free time. He's maintained he wanted to make the most of his free time before Callum or I had kids, because when and if that happens, he wants to be a hands on papa because it's what my mum would've wanted.

He's right about that.

Mum would have been an amazing nana. I give myself a pep talk about today; I don't want to be thinking sad thoughts. My mum had an amazing life and did so much for others over the years; these are the memories I should keep firmly at the forefront of my mind.

"Ella, are you okay?" Trevor's voice brings me back to reality as we pull up outside the hotel where we're meeting the CEO.

"Yes, sorry. I was a million miles away thinking about Mum."

"You're very much like your mum. Headstrong, determined, and beautiful. But even Sheena would've been disappointed with how you handled the Donovan situation. Can I tell you something else?"

"Please do."

"Your mum never thought you'd end up with Donovan. She

had told Betty on more than one occasion she'd seen the likes of him before. She said she already knew the man that would one day win your heart."

"Who is that?"

"Betty has kept that to herself. You would have to ask her yourself, but I do have my suspicions. Now, come on. Let's go and meet this man."

He smirks, getting out of the car, and I find myself grinning at thoughts of my mum and Betty gossiping over a cup tea about who I would end up with. Would she be happy about me and Connor? I find myself smirking. Of course she would. If everyone else knew how Connor felt about me, I'm sure she knew too. I exit the car, and Trevor tells the driver to come back in an hour and a half.

We enter the hotel and Trevor leads the way to the bar, which isn't busy, but there are a few people sitting around having tea and coffee. There's two men sitting by the windows with no one else near them. One man is in a suit the other in jeans and a t-shirt. The man in the suit stands as we approach his table. He's maybe a few years older than me, and very handsome. "Trevor, good to meet you," he says, holding his hand out to Trevor.

"Likewise. Ella, this is Martin Brown. Martin, Miss Ella Mc-Gregor."

Martin kisses me on the cheek. "It's lovely to meet you, Miss McGregor."

"Please, just Ella. Nice to meet you too."

"This is Will. He's our photographer."

"A pleasure to meet you, Will."

"The pleasure is all mine, I can assure you," he says with a thick Scottish accent, putting me at ease.

We take a seat and order tea and coffee from a waiter. "Ella, my company is hugely successful because we don't compromise on quality or style when it comes to our products. We are affordable to everyone. We are a far cry from the designer brands but we compete well with other high street stores. The sudden spike of interest and sales in my business is truly incredible. I never thought a movie star like you would shop in any of my stores, but to pick one of our dresses and wear it to a premiere . . . I'm truly flattered."

"Martin, can I be truthful?" He nods and I look to Trevor. He smiles as he has an idea of what I'm about to say. "Things have happened recently that have made me sit back and re-evaluate my whole life. I won't go into it all because I'm sure you'll read about it. I stumbled into your store and was impressed with what I saw. I made a conscious decision that I wasn't spending thousands of pounds on a dress in a designer boutique."

"Well, I'm glad you did. As I've said, there has been a lot of interest in my business, including lots of online sales of the dress you wore, which resulted in my website crashing yesterday."

"Oh."

"It's all good and back up and running. Although, that dress is now completely out of stock." I smile. "Let's talk about today's photoshoot, and there are a few events I would love you to attend in London in the coming weeks."

I sit quietly and listen as Martin tells me all about his plans for driving his business forward and, as I listen to him talk enthusiastically about it, I'm really privileged to be working for him and his business. I get what he wants to do and achieve, which is provide an affordable fashion range for everyone.

As he talks about today's fashion shoot that will be featured both online and on his store magazine, I really wish I wasn't so thin at the moment.

"This is all very exciting, but can I ask a question?" Martin nods. "Why women's fashion?"

"This was a joint business between my wife and me. We started with the online shop about ten years ago and built it from there. This was her passion."

"Was?" I'm dreading hearing the answer.

"My wife passed away last year, leaving me and our daughter."

"I'm so sorry. What age is your daughter?"

"She's only five." He reaches into the inside of his suit jacket, taking out his wallet, and opens it. He takes a picture from it and hands it over to me.

"She's beautiful. She looks like her mum," I say as I hand it back to him. I can't imagine losing my mum when I was that young. Not having her around to talk about all the first things that happened in my life as a teen; periods, boys, all the usual stuff. My heart breaks for Martin as I think about that.

"Thank you. I'm sure she's going to be a handful as she grows up."

"Just as much as this one then," Trevor says with a warm smile. I can't argue with what he's said.

"So, my daughter and my wife are my driving force behind making this business a success. Lately, so many big businesses have gone out of business. I want to continue to strive forward and if, one day, my daughter wants to take over then it will all be hers. If not, she'll be free to sell it as a going concern. As for my wife, I just want it to work out because this was her hopes and dreams and she couldn't see it out for herself."

"I'm sure your wife is very proud of you."

"Okay, if we're all finished, let's go and pick up some clothes for you, and Will can start taking some pictures."

We all travel together in Trevor's car to the city centre store. Will and I talk about what he wants to achieve from the shoot. He asks if he can take a couple of extra shots to add to his business portfolio. I agree after a quick chat with Trevor who is in a deep conversation with Martin.

As we enter the store, lots of shoppers stop to see what is going on. Voices are hushed as they try to guess. In the store, I leave the guys talking to the shop manager while I wander around, looking for the perfect outfits to model.

This is new to me. I've done photoshoots before, but this seems different. Will follows behind me and I already know he's snapping away on his camera; I don't need to turn around to know that.

I smile and say hello to a few customers in store who stare in my direction. A little black dress catches my eye and I hold it up. Will moves and I can see him before me. "What do you think?" I ask him.

"I'm not sure I should say considering you're not a single woman."

I shake my head. "Should I include it?"

"Hell yes." I now know what he thinks of the dress. "Ella, some of the pictures I've got look so natural as you look through the clothes. I've also had an idea that I'd like to run past Martin."

"What's that?"

"There's some really amazing buildings around here I'd like to get a few shots of you in front of. I had planned to take lots of shots inside the store, but it's a lovely day. The light is perfect and I'm sure we could do a lot outside. The only thing that concerns me is your privacy. You won't get that."

I glance around the store. "What privacy?" Will looks around and there's more than a few people with their phones in their hands.

"I see what you mean," he says with a smile. Will reminds me of Callum, a little.

"Have you found anything?" Trevor asks, joining us.

"Yes, a few things."

"Martin has said he's happy to close the store if having shoppers is distracting you."

"No, it's fine. Anyway, Will wants to take some shots outside."

"As long as you are happy about that. You are my main concern today, Ella. I promised your dad I would look after you."

"And you're keeping that promise. If anything gets too much, I promise to tell you. Now, I should go and change." I head off to the changing room, following the manager that was here the other day. I'm so glad Julie came over and did my hair and make-up for me this morning, otherwise I wouldn't have a good look going on. The manager took the clothes I picked from me and said she would get a few more outfits. Some new stock. She hangs everything in the same large changing room I've already been in.

I change into the black dress and it looks better on than it did on the hanger. With a certain amount of confidence, I leave the changing room. Trevor is with Martin and Will, standing to my left, and he instantly starts snapping away on the camera.

Trevor is a Godsend. Why I never had him as my agent before now still baffles me. Oh, yes. I had that complete prick Donovan Bell.

"Ella, darling, you look beautiful as always," he says, walking toward me.

"Thanks, but you've got to say that."

"I don't and I always tell you the truth. Now, where are we going first?" Trevor asks Will and Martin.

"Outside."

TODAY'S PHOTOSHOOT HAS been fun but exhausting. I've had more costume changes than I would have for an entire shoot on a movie set, but I loved every minute of it. Will was great to work with. He made me feel so relaxed, especially when we were outside and it felt like everybody in Glasgow city centre was watching.

I can't wait to see what he's got. Some of his shots from me looking through the shop rails have already been uploaded to the store's social media. They look good, and if the constant buzzing of my phone is an indication, it would seem they are causing as much of a stir for the company as it did after the premiere.

My phone beeps in my hand.

Connor: I hope you're hungry x

Me: Yes and no. I'm really tired x

Connor: I picked up pizza x

Me: I'm sure I can manage a few slices x

Connor: Is that all you'll manage???

Me: Oh I don't know. What else do you have in mind? X

Connor: Now that would be telling. I saw some pictures. You look amazing. See you soon x

With thoughts of Connor in my head, I sit back and enjoy the journey back home alone. Trevor wanted to get home. I don't think either of us realised how long today would be. But, I would do it all again tomorrow.

Connor had wanted to come with me today, but he would've been a distraction. Now, I can't wait to see him and fall into his arms.

Chapter 19

"TEA OR COFFEE," I SHOUT up the stairs, hoping Connor hears me. He really needs to hurry up or he'll be running late. He has a meeting with Trevor this morning and, this afternoon, we're meeting with the production team of the soap opera and I can honestly say we're both excited. Everything about this project appeals to us.

Working at home in Scotland has already sealed the deal in my mind. Life here goes at a much slower pace than it does in L.A., and if I'm truthful with myself, I was sick of all the parties Donovan dragged me along to. Some weeks, we were out every night, and when you're working long shifts on set, it begins to take its toll. No wonder all I longed for was home.

And as for Connor, he feels the same way. He would much rather be here, but will go wherever he needs to go for work.

This past week has been non-stop. I had completely forgotten how easy it is to get caught up in everything going on around me. The feelings of excitement about an industry that I'm blessed to be a part of have returned. I'm buzzing to read through some of the projects I've been linked with and some of them are in the UK.

My phone hasn't stopped ringing since Connor's premiere. Not only have I done the photoshoot for Inspire, but I'll be heading to London in the coming weeks to do another photoshoot for them and someone will be filming some behind-the-scenes footage that they hope to use on the television. I'm excited about that.

Connor has just as much going on as I do. He's been asked to do a commercial for a new brand of aftershave. We're hoping we can tie them both in at the same time as we need to be in London.

I can't help but smile with thoughts of Connor in my head. He's given me a new lease of life. He's inspired my passion that had long since gone about acting. And now I'm really excited about working alongside him.

There's still been nothing from Donovan, and even though I've tried to push it to the back of my mind, there's a lingering thought that he's up to something. Although, what it is, I don't know. So until I hear from him, I'm just going to enjoy my life because, even with all I've been through lately, life is good and I still want to help others.

Footsteps bring my attention back to here and now. "Neither, I've no time," Connor says, walking down the stairs. "I'll need to go. Can I take your car?"

I cast my eyes over him as he reaches me. He looks pretty good in black jeans and a tight cream sweater. "Oh, I don't know. The last time you drove my car you upset us both." Our day at the beach, I swear he thought he was on a race track the way he took some of the corners on the country roads.

A day out at a race track could be the perfect present for his birthday next month. I've been thinking about this for days; what do you get someone who has everything? I think it's the perfect present for him.

He takes a step closer to me and dips his head, his lips almost touching mine. "What if I promise to look after you both?" His words whisper across my skin. "What do you say?" His lips touch mine delicately.

"I could be persuaded."

"I know you could. Now, have you given any more thought

to going to L.A.?"

He's asked this question repeatedly since I told him the producers of a new movie want to meet with me as soon as possible. This is the same movie that Katherine Hunter has also been shortlisted for. "I still don't know." The thought of being in L.A. isn't sitting well with me.

"Ella, I understand your fears, really I do, but you have to do this. If you go to L.A, I wouldn't let you go alone. I would be right there beside you to hold your hand. But, I think you have the strength to do it."

"My reservations aren't just about Donovan, or Katherine, for that matter. It's more to do with the fact that I don't want to split my time between two countries. My home is here in Scotland. I have no desire to go back to spending half the year across the Atlantic because of filming schedules."

He wraps his arms around me and I allow my hands to rest on his shoulders. "I get that. There's no rush for a decision. We can see what the production crew have to say to us this afternoon."

This is what I'm most excited about work wise; the soap opera. For me, it ticks all the right boxes and means I can stay where I want; at home.

"Thank you."

"What for?"

"For not pushing me into making a rash decision."

I lift my head and find myself looking into his eyes. "I won't ever push you into doing something you're not comfortable with, especially when it comes to your career. I'll always support you in every decision you have to make."

I kiss him briefly. "You'd better go if you want to get there on time."

"Yeah, I should. So can I take your car? And I'll pick you up so we can go to the meeting together."

"Yes, go on before I make you late for Trevor."

"Promises, promises." He gives me a kiss before turning, grabbing my car keys, and walking out the front door. My eyes linger on the door until I hear my car engine roar to life. With a shake of my head, I make my way back through the house into the kitchen to make myself a cup of tea.

MY CAR HORN startles me. I walk over and look out of the window. Connor waves at me from the driver's seat. He looks as though he has no intention of swapping seats and letting me drive. He had better have been kind to my wee car today because, if he hasn't, I'll know. I grab my bag along with the script I've been reading and leave the house.

My phone buzzes in my hand as I lock the front door. I glance down at the screen.

Shit.

No.

Donovan Bell.

Panic races through my body, making it hard for me to breathe. Everything around me begins to look blurry. I'm going to pass out. How the hell can a man who hasn't been a part of my life for over three months have such a dramatic effect on me? This is silly, I know it is, but I can't help myself.

I can't turn around. I can't move from the spot. My body shakes, tears fill my eyes, and I haven't even opened his message. Two weeks since the pictures of Connor and me went public. That's how long he's waited to make his move. A move I knew would come.

He waited until the perfect time, for maximum effect.

Everything was going too well in my life.

The car door bangs closed and I hear Connor's footsteps rush toward me, but I still can't find the energy to move.

"Ella! Ella, what's wrong." He places his arms around me and turns me to face him. He's there before me, I feel him, but can't see him. My vision has stopped working and all I see is Donovan Bell with a smug face because he thinks he has one over on me.

Connor wipes away my falling tears before taking my phone out of my hand. Silence descends and I know he's opened the message and he's reading it.

"Ella, it's okay. I have you." He wraps both arms around me and pulls me close to him. My trembling legs stumble toward him and he rubs my back, comforting me.

"What does it say?" I ask after a few minutes.

"It says he wants to talk to you, that's all." That can't be all he wants. There has to be more to it. He's playing games and he only plays games that he thinks he can win. I should know; I've watched him play enough games over the last five years.

"Ella, come on. You need to breathe slowly. Here, sit down." He lowers me to the step and moves position so he's kneeling in front of me, holding my hands. I do as he asks and breathe slowly over and over, bringing me back from my panic-induced state. "There's my girl."

"Sorry," I mutter.

"Hey, you've nothing to be sorry for."

"Is that really all his text message says?" I ask. He nods, holding the phone up so I can read it for myself. "And here I've worked myself into such a panic. How the hell am I going to cope when I need to come face-to-face with him?"

"Ella, stop thinking. Just concentrate on now. He doesn't deserve to be in your thoughts. He's messing with you. We both knew he would start doing it sooner rather than later. You need to keep your smile in place and not let him see he's getting to you." I know Connor is right, but with Donovan's sudden message, I feel as though I've taken two steps backwards when my life should be moving forward. "You have so much to look forward to. Now, if you're ready, we should get going. We don't want to keep our new employers waiting." I smile at his words and allow him to pull me back up to my feet and toward the car.

I get in at the passenger side. After all my internal moaning about Connor driving my car, I'm in no fit state to drive it. My poor car. "Everything will be okay, I promise," Connor says, getting into the driver's seat. I nod, hoping he's right. But I also know Donovan, very well, and I'm certain this won't be the last I hear from him.

"OKAY, NOW WE'RE alone, you can tell me your thoughts," Trevor says as we sit in this quiet café.

I smile at Connor. "I'm impressed with everything they've offered and I love the storyline that will introduce us," I tell him. I will be introduced as a love child of one of the leading characters. Connor is going to play someone who works for my dad. It really does sound amazing.

"Connor, what about you? You're very quiet." He looks deep in thought as Trevor and I watch him.

"Sorry. I'd never heard about this programme until I received the proposal, but I'm impressed. They're very professional. And I can't get over their viewing figures. I think we need to start watching it to bring ourselves up to speed on all the current storylines before we start filming."

I can't believe in five weeks' time we start filming, or rather, I do. Connor will join the cast two weeks later. We met a few cast members today and they all seem really nice. I even met the man who will play my dad. After being told about his on-screen character—in the eyes of the viewers a baddie—he's really quite sweet.

"I'm really pleased you're both happy with everything. Now, we have a few other things to discuss. I've managed to arrange for you to be in London at the same time. So the commercial for Inspire and the aftershave one will be filmed over the same weekend. So you should pack for going away on Thursday morning. Hotel and flights are booked. Don't say I'm not good to you."

"That's fantastic," I say, now having a weekend away with Connor to look forward to.

Trevor goes on to tell us that we've been invited to a movie premiere and after party on Thursday night.

"Neither of you will be able to party hard because you'll both be filming on Friday. Hopefully, it will get wrapped up on Friday and then Saturday and Sunday you'll be free to do what you want. I'll be traveling with you so I can keep an eye on the filming. That will be hard with you being in different locations, but I'm sure we'll work it out."

Trevor will look out and work hard for us, of that I have no doubt. On the off chance he didn't look out for me, he'd have Dad to answer to.

Today, many things have dawned on me. I love my life, almost every aspect of it. I have great family and friends who support me unconditionally. Yes, I might be ready to move on in so many ways; new man, new and exciting job opportunities, but I've learned I'm still vulnerable when it comes to Donovan. And I've decided that's okay because it means where he is concerned, I'll always be on my guard.

I'm so glad I was able to put my wobble earlier behind me because I've enjoyed my day. Now I'm more than excited about what the future holds for me.

Chapter 20

"I'M SURE I SAID SOMETHING about taking care of you." Connor's words whisper delicately across the back of my neck. Goosebumps spread along my skin. My eyes close as his arms thread under mine and wrap around my waist.

"Mmm, yes you did," I say breathlessly, unable to say anything else as I enjoy the warm, fuzzy feelings spreading through my body. His hands rest against my stomach. In moments like this, I feel as though it's all a dream. I worry that if I wake up, he'll be gone, leaving a void in my life.

We're in the hallway, sexual tension charged between us, but yet, there's the gentleness that I've grown used to these past two weeks. Being with Connor makes me feel relaxed. He makes me feel wanted and desired all the time. I stand in front of him with my heart hammering in my chest, not wanting to take a step away from him. I'm enjoying the feel of him beside me.

"Ella, turn around," he orders gently, and I comply without hesitation. I open my eyes and slowly turn in his arms. His eyes are focused on me. "Today has been incredible, hearing your passion and excitement for a profession I thought you had given up on, but now I plan on fulfilling my promise to you earlier."

"You also promised to take care of my car," I say, teasing him.

"And, I think you'll find I did. I took extra care with your car.

Now, it's your turn." He leans forward, dipping his head. His lips touch mine. "For the rest of tonight, I plan to take care of you and enjoy every last inch of your incredible body."

I'm where I want to be; in the arms of an amazing man who only wants me. His tongue skims my bottom lip, seeking entry, and I can't deny him. Our tongues collide as his mouth crushes against mine. I throw my arms over his shoulders and his grip tightens around my waist, holding me close. His erection presses against my lower stomach.

I want him as much, if not more, than he wants me.

A low moan escapes his mouth as he slides his hands up my back and takes hold of my hair, bunching it in his hands and tugging gently, pulling my head back a little. "I've watched you all afternoon, longing to touch you. Needing to feel your body beneath mine. I've sat back and admired you when you thought I wasn't paying attention. You, Ella McGregor, held everyone's attention when we were in meetings today and you never even noticed. You never noticed that each person in that room was, like me, hanging on every word you said. Now, though, it's just you and me. No distractions."

"Take me to bed."

"Yes, mam. You don't have to tell me twice." He takes my hand. We climb the stairs and he pauses outside his bedroom. His eyes dart to the master bedroom opposite his; I wish I knew what he was thinking. He opens his bedroom door and tugs on my hand, pulling me into the room with him.

With a bang, he kicks the door closed.

He lets go of my hand and stands before me. I reach up, running my fingers over the coarse stubble on his face; it's comforting beneath the palms of my hands and I press my lips to his. He wraps his arms around me, pulling my body tight against his. And in this moment, I know I'll never get enough of him. I lean my forehead against his. "There's no going back," I whisper.

"Ella, for me there was never a way back, only forward with you. It's the only reason I've stuck around all these years. I had hope."

His lips capture mine, our mouths joining in a kiss that holds so much emotion. So much passion flowing between us. He's right; we can only go forward in our lives. The need for him intensifies. Every nerve ending in my body is on high alert, wanting more, wanting his touch. My body wants him to claim me.

Who am I kidding? He's already claimed me as his.

He pulls back, breaking our kiss, and I want to cry out in protest at our broken connection. I take him in. His eyes glisten and then my eyes move down his perfect face, stopping on his lips that, after a few seconds, curl at the corners, knocking me off balance. His fingertips dance gently across my back and everything about this moment tells me he's trying to tell me something.

"Ella, let me make love to you?" I hear the slight quiver in his voice as he asks the question. I nod, because his question has left me breathless. I close my eyes as my body trembles at what this means. In his own way he's telling me how he feels about me, but in a way that won't scare me off.

He knows I need time *and* patience and he's prepared to give me both.

I open my eyes as he starts to undress me. He's in no rush, taking his time to enjoy and savour this moment. He's not the only one. Every piece of my clothing he removes, he stands and carefully folds it, placing it down on a chest of drawers.

I stand before him, completely naked and unashamed, and watch as he undresses and carefully puts his own clothes in a neat pile beside mine.

He walks toward me, scoops me up into his arms, and I let out a squeal as he marches with purpose toward his bed. Connor places me down in the centre of the bed, almost as carefully as he folded our clothes.

He lowers himself onto the bed above me, leaning his head down and teasing my lips with the whisper of a kiss and slowly pushes inside me.

There's more between us tonight than just the physical connection we've shared recently. There's a bond, I feel it. All the way to the depths of my soul. I watch as his eyes cloud with desire and darken with love as he slides deeper inside me.

Love.

Sensations flood me, like a river pulling me under. I see darkness and light, uncertainty and surprises, hope and fear, but I don't feel frightened. I feel alive and free.

He groans as he starts to move. My body reacts instinctively, my back arching. I push my hips up to meet him.

The feel of his skin against mine. The gentle caress of his fingers on my face. The undeniable love in his eyes. The soft groan of pleasure . . . It's all too much, yet not enough. Tears fill my eyes, but not of sadness. It's because of the amount of happiness Connor has brought into my life. He's pulled me out from the quicksand I was drowning under and brought a ray of light into my life when darkness was all I saw.

A rush of heat engulfs me as he grinds his hips, ensuring I feel him deeper, before slowly pulling back out and doing it all again.

My body vibrates beneath his as pressure builds, leaving me dizzy. Connor has set a slow and steady pace that allows him to draw out the sensual high that is sending me spiralling on a collision course.

With his eyes still holding mine, I see I'm not the only one heading down a one-way street. We're both on the same journey. His pleasure spikes, his jaw tightens in concentration, his heavy eyelids close briefly. His nostrils flare as he attempts to take several deep breaths.

"Connor . . ." I moan. The spark of ignition sends heat racing through my body. My muscles tense. He shifts position, sitting back on his knees, sliding his hands down both sides of my body. The smallest of touches has me lost in the onslaught of sensations that sweep through my burning body.

"The look on your face right now; I'll never tire of seeing it. Watching you fall apart beneath me is my favourite pastime. Can you carry on?" I nod because I'm not capable of speaking. I'm sure if I tried to reply it would only come out in a slurred mess.

With his grip now firmly on my hips, he holds me in place. I tilt my hips as he continues to push in and then withdraw, leaving me wanting more each time. My senses are still on high alert after my orgasm. I try to refocus my attention back to him, but it's hard when my body surges forward, anticipating another release. He's driving me higher and higher and I'm almost at the point of no return. My thighs tighten and all I want to do is close my eyes and enjoy the feelings that will sweep through my body.

He stops.

I stare at him in frustration for stealing my moment. Leaving me wanting and waiting.

He smiles.

He surges forward, pushing deeper inside, and I moan. Pushing my thighs back, he hits that sweet spot that is sometimes beyond his reach, but in this position, everything is well within reach. My eyes close and this time I can't keep them open. He pounds into me recklessly, driving us both to the brink.

"You are my heaven and hell combined," he says, leaning forward and pressing his lips to mine. Pushing his tongue between my lips, he dominates our kiss just the same as he dominates the pace he's set. His restraint is slipping away, just as mine has already done.

He rocks deeper into me and the fire within me starts to spread at a lightning pace. My body begins to tremble from the punishing rhythm. Our joined moans fill the room. Mindless pleasure consumes me as I surrender to the orgasm that takes me captive.

He doesn't still, but pushes on, pounding deep into me, over and over. I open my eyes just at the right moment. His body tenses, his eyes close, and I feel him. All of him.

"Ella," he growls.

He rolls us to our sides, but we stay connected. I hold him close, not wanting to lose what we've just shared. Our pounding hearts and ragged breathing are all that can be heard amongst the silence. It's comforting.

"I should move," I say after a few minutes.

"You are going nowhere. I'm not nearly done with you. I told you I planned to take care of you all night long and that's what I intend to do."

Who am I to argue with that?

Chapter 21

"I CAN'T BELIEVE YOU'RE IN London and I'm stuck home alone," Julie whines through the phone in between her coughing and sneezing. I hold it away from my ear and Connor laughs, shaking his head as we enter our hotel room. "Ella, I'm not kidding."

Her nose is out of joint because I'm here with Connor. She loves these events. She can always be found mingling with all the celebrities, especially the single ones. She was invited, but she declined, given the fact that she's loaded with a cold. "You two have your fun. Don't worry about me," she says sniffling.

"Okay, we won't." I know she's teasing. She's happy we managed to get away together.

"Ella McGregor, you witch. But I know you'll have a great time."

"I'll try. Look, I'd better go. We're at our room and I don't have long before we need to leave."

"Okay. There's someone coming to do your hair and make-up in about . . . oh, half an hour. You can thank me when you see me during the week. Maybe lunch?"

Why does this not surprise me? She is so thoughtful. I'm okay at doing my make-up and hair, but it's nowhere near professional standards. "Thank you, and yes, we'll do lunch. Love you."

"Yeah, yeah. Now go and have fun." We end our call.

I walk through the room toward the bed, dropping my phone on it. Trevor has done good, although I wouldn't expect anything else from him. But, I'm surprised he didn't bring up sleeping arrangements to me before we left Glasgow. This suite is incredible. It feels cool yet warm with its soft greys and deep reds. All very sensual.

I walk over to the large sash bay windows and I'm staring straight out onto Piccadilly Circus. Right in the heart of London. Maybe I should find out what shows are on in the theatres and Connor and I can have a proper date.

"What are you thinking?" Connor asks, approaching me from behind and securely wrapping his arms around my body and resting them on my stomach.

"I'm thinking the room is perfect but I'm a little surprised Trevor didn't book two rooms."

"He did, but I very politely asked him to change the reservation."

"I see."

"Yes, you do. If only we had more time to ourselves before we have to leave," he whispers against my ear.

"We don't, but I'm sure the wait until you get me in that bed will be worth it."

"Of that I have no doubts. I'm going to call for some room service and order us some sandwiches because neither of us has eaten since breakfast and there's no way I'm letting you drink on an empty stomach. So go and shower before whoever Julie has organised is here."

I turn in his arms. "You knew?"

"Of course." He presses the briefest kiss to my lips and releases his hold of me. I stand and watch as he picks up the telephone and orders food and a bottle of wine. I leave him and wander through the suite until I find myself in the most amazing bathroom. Everything in here is brilliant white with a few red accessories thrown in. My eyes take in the giant bath tub that looks as though it would fit two comfortably. A relaxing bath with a bottle of fizz does sound appealing.

Shaking my thoughts from my head, I undress, switch the shower on, and stand under the warm flowing water. *Perfect*. Just what I need to wash away a day full of travelling. With our flight being delayed today, we would've been quicker travelling by train.

I'm looking forward to being out and about tonight, but I'm also a little nervous. I should've asked Trevor to check out the guest list for me. Voices in the other room grab my attention and I wonder if it's room service or the hairdresser and make-up artist. I suppose that means I should get out.

Switching the water off, I shiver, suddenly feeling cold. I grab a large white fluffy towel and quickly dry myself before putting on the dressing gown and leaving the bathroom.

Room service has been delivered. So much for just some sandwiches; there's enough food on the table for a party. Along with my favourite; a bottle of champagne.

Connor exits the bedroom and joins me with my phone in his hand. There's no smile on his face, no glint in his eye, and I know something is wrong.

I freeze.

Donovan.

That's the only explanation.

He's not contacted me again since the other day, but given the grim expression on Connor's face, that's changed. "What's wrong?" I ask nervously, not sure if I want the answer.

"He's been back in touch," Connor says, moving toward me.

"What does he say?"

"He sounds a bit more desperate than his message earlier in the week. He really needs to speak with you. Each message is the same."

"What do you mean, each message is the same?"

"He's sent ten messages in as many minutes."

Shit! That does sound desperate. "I don't care how desperate he is. I'm not getting back to him. I'm not interested in anything he has to say." I take a seat at the table and don't wait to see the expression on Connor's face. Yes, he's bound to be concerned, but I don't want Donovan Bell to put a damper on tonight or this weekend. I open the champagne without looking in his direction.

"Are we not going to talk about this?"

"No."

"Ella . . ."

"Don't. I don't want us to have an argument over him. Please. I don't want him to come between us or ruin the weekend."

He moves closer to me, resting his hand on my shoulder. I tilt my head back, looking directly into his amazing eyes. "I can promise you, he will never come between us." He takes the bottle from my hands and fills up the glasses before us. "A toast! To an amazing weekend with an equally amazing woman." He hands me a glass and we clink our glasses before taking a drink.

"To an amazing weekend with a wonderful man." He takes the seat opposite me and has the biggest smile on his face. He places my phone face down on the table. I'm sure it will buzz again, but I'm not interested. We eat in silence, a comfortable understanding filling the air around us, until there's a knock on the door.

"That will be Julie's friend here to work her magic."

"Hey, cheeky," I say, reaching over and playfully slapping his arm.

He stands and walks around the table. "You know I don't mean it."

I raise my eyebrows and watch as he wanders toward the door and opens it. A young woman enters, pulling a small trolley behind her. I smile as Connor shows her through to the bedroom.

"She's setting up. I'll get ready in here and leave you in peace." He's very thoughtful. I'm glad because I don't want him to see my dress until I'm in it. "Go on. Go and get pampered. You deserve it."

I STAND IN front of the mirror, feeling giddy as I take in my appearance. Long gone is the woman who stared back at me almost three weeks ago. So much has changed in such a short period, least of all the small fact that I've put on some of the weight I'd lost. It's only a small amount, but I look so much healthier and happier. The happiness is all Connor's doing. I can't take any of the credit for that.

My hair is incredible, all curled and hanging loosely down my back and framing my face. It really does look more blonde than light brown now, and I love the colour of it. The make-up is light, yet effective. The lady Julie organised has done an amazing job with both, and she was lovely.

I'm struggling to take in my figure in this tight gold dress that sits just below the knee; some of my curves are back and I can't believe how good I look. Turning to the side to see how the back looks, I see it's really low with lots of skin on show.

I slip my feet into my black Jimmy Choos, add my jewellery, and pick up my black matching clutch bag that contains the essentials; my bank card, lipstick, and my perfume.

With a deep breath, I leave the bedroom.

Bloody hell.

And I thought Connor looked handsome in his kilt at his own premiere. He looks amazing in his dark suit, white shirt, and dark tie. I smile, thinking he's worn that to match my shoes. He must've seen my shoes and bag before we left home to pick out a tie almost identical in colour. He shaved a few days ago, much to my disappointment, but there's now a slight shadow along his jawline. Connor looks hot.

Deliciously hot.

"Wow, you look amazing," he says, taking a step toward me,

his eyes roaming my entire body.

"So, I pass then?"

"Babe, of course you do. I can't wait to show you off, have you on my arm, and also be the man you leave the after party with. Bring you back to that bed next door and make passionate love to you all night long."

I gulp, swallowing hard at his last statement.

"We need to leave," he says, sounding somewhat reluctant. "Our car is waiting downstairs." He pauses for a moment before adding, "All I want to do is take you in my arms and kiss you."

"Please don't do that. I don't have Julie or her friend here to do last minute touch-ups."

"Okay, but you'd better put this in your bag," he says, handing me my phone.

"Has there been . . ."

"No. Nothing else."

I sigh heavily, relieved I can go and enjoy my night and the company of a very sexy and hot Scotsman.

Connor's eyes travel down my body, smiling in appreciation, and back up until his eyes meet mine. "Let's go and have some fun."

Chapter 22

FUN!

He has no idea.

Connor wants to have fun tonight and I'm sure we can have a lot if this limo is booked to collect us at the end of the night. The journey isn't long from the hotel to the venue, but I'm now hoping we can persuade the driver to take the long, scenic route back to our hotel.

"We're nearly there," Connor says.

"So I see." The streets outside are busy; nothing unusual for any night of the week in London. It's always busy. Life moves at such a fast pace here; everyone always seems to be in a hurry.

Ringing from my bag draws my attention away from the windows. My eyes dart to Connor and I'm sure it's my own worried expression I see reflecting from him.

Slowly, I open my bag, and relief sweeps through me when I see Trevor's name flashing across the screen.

"Hi, Trevor," I say answering the call and looking at Connor.

"Hi. Ella. Have you heard from Donovan?"

"What's wrong?" I ask, panic in my voice. Connor takes my free hand, holding it tightly in his, rubbing his thumb in circles against mine.

"I need to know."

"He sent a text at the start of the week and today sent ten messages in a short space of time and, before you ask, I've not replied to any of them. What's wrong?"

"Ella, Donovan is in London." My heart sinks. "I wasn't coming to the premiere but I'm here now. I'll be waiting for you. How long until . . ." I don't hear anything else; I've zoned out. He's going to be here tonight. I know it. Why else would he be in London? I drop my phone but it doesn't fall into my lap.

"Trevor, we're only a few minutes away . . . No, she'll be fine . . . See you soon."

He ends the call and I turn to face him. "Ella, tell me what you're thinking."

"That I want to go home because I'm scared of how I'll react in public if I come face-to-face with him. But there's also a part of me that's telling me not to be so stupid and not allow him to see that he's affecting my life."

"There's my girl. You have the strength to do this, but most of all, you have my support to get through this. Trevor says Donovan's name isn't on the guest list, but Katherine Hunter's name is."

Of course he'll accompany her tonight. Why wouldn't he after all the time they've spent together recently? I nod slowly, not trusting my mouth to say the words that are spinning around in my head. Like, can we turn around and go straight back to the hotel room? That sounds like a great plan. I know Connor would be able to distract me for the rest of the night.

The car stops and I can already see a heavy security presence around the venue along with the ever present British media.

"Are you ready? Trevor is waiting just to the side for us."

"Yes, I'm ready. You'll be by my side the whole night?"

"Yes."

Someone opens the car doors and we exit at the same time. Flashing lights blind me momentarily. Connor is quickly by my side, wrapping his arm around me. I look at him and smile. "See?

You can do this."

"Mr Andrews. Miss McGregor." Our names are called out and we stand in front of the waiting media. Cameras flash from all directions, but having Connor by my side is comforting. We pose for a few photos before making our way along the red carpet, where Trevor is waiting at the entrance.

Calmness sweeps through me when I see the smile on Trevor's face. In this moment, I take comfort as he looks more relaxed than I expected. He takes a step forward as we reach him, and opens his arms. Connor releases his hold of me and I step into the familiar, loving embrace of Trevor.

"Sweetheart, everything is okay. He's not here."

"Really? How do you know?"

"Because Katherine arrived ten minutes ago with one of her friends."

I smile and kiss him on the cheek before he lets me go and Connor wraps his arm back around my waist. "Let's go and enjoy our night," Connor says, leading the way inside.

Trevor stays close beside us and that pleases me. I think I'll need their strength when I come face-to-face with Katherine Hunter. The one thing I've learned about her over the years is that she can't be trusted. She's devious and will hurt anyone who gets in her way when she wants something.

A waiter with a tray of glasses approaches and Connor hands Trevor and me a glass of champagne each before taking one for himself. Everyone who is anyone in the industry is already here. Looks as though lots of big names have flown in from the States. Connor and Trevor stand beside me, talking, and I'm not paying attention to a word either of them is saying.

My eyes scan the area and I see a lot of familiar and friendly faces in the crowd. Then I see her. Katherine Hunter is standing by the bar with her friend, a drink in her hand. She's looking around the room nervously. She doesn't seem as composed as

I've seen her in the past.

She stops; her eyes stare straight at me. I watch her as she anxiously moves from one foot to the other. She looks physically shaken as recognition hits her. I don't turn or shy away; I raise my glass and offer her a smile. She doesn't return it. Instead, she turns back to her friend.

"Well done," Connor says, bringing my attention back to him. I smile. "Are you okay?"

"You know what? I am."

"Glad to hear it," says Trevor. "Now, if you follow me, I want to personally introduce you to the casting director of the movie you've been shortlisted for."

"Should I be nervous?"

I'm surprised that it's Connor who answers my question. "You have nothing to be nervous about. If they don't love you, that's their problem, not yours." Trevor nods in agreement.

We make our way through the crowded room, getting stopped along the way with colleagues and friends wanting to talk to Connor and me. All the time we spend talking with other actors and producers, I find myself glancing in Katherine's direction, and the one thing I notice is that she looks reluctant and a bit scared to engage in conversation with anyone except her friend.

"YOU TWO GO and enjoy the party. Don't make it too late a night, remember. I'll collect you from the hotel at ten a.m, Ella."

"I won't forget." I give him a hug and thank him for everything before he leaves.

"Okay, it's just us. What do you say we skip the after party?" Connor asks as we stand at the bar.

"I say we mingle here for a bit then I'm all yours for the rest of the night."

"That sounds like a perfect plan." His eyes roam the room.

"Is there anyone you want to meet?"

"Not really, although I do feel I need to go and talk to Katherine Hunter."

"Are you sure?" he asks, his voice full of concern.

"Yes." I need to do this for me.

"Okay then. Let's go and introduce you to Miss Hunter." With a quick deep breath, I square my shoulders back, hold my head high, and walk toward her with Connor by my side.

She doesn't see us approaching her. "Katherine, I thought I should come over and at least introduce myself."

She turns around hesitantly, staring at me in total bewilderment. "Oh! Hi, Ella." Her voice is rough with what I think is anxiety.

"Katherine, this is Connor."

"Hi."

"So, you and Ella have been shortlisted for the same part."

"So I've been told," she says, her tone heavy with sarcasm. Me standing here is making her uncomfortable. "Will you be coming to L.A.?"

"No, the casting producer is happy to see me this weekend. Here in London."

"Oh," she says, her voice cold.

"What about you? How long are you in the UK for?"

"We're not sure. We have a few things to do and I'd like to catch up with an old friend." We? And I presume the old friend she's talking about is Alex Mathews.

"Has Donovan got work here?" I ask, putting her on the spot. I glance at Connor and I think I've surprised him with my question.

"Erm, yes. He has a few things he has to take care of." She might be speaking to me but her eyes are scanning the room, looking for the nearest exit. Inwardly, I find myself laughing. "It was great to meet you both. If you're coming to the after party, I'm sure you'll be able to catch up with Donovan then."

Connor fidgets beside me and I know he's wondering how I'm going to react, but he has nothing to worry about. There will be no tears or shouting from me, although I can't guarantee the same for Katherine Hunter. "That would've been great," I say. "But we have plans. If you could pass on a message to him for me though, I would appreciate it. Tell him to stop messaging me. If he wants anything, he should contact Trevor or Jonathon, my lawyer."

She stands before me, her eyes almost popping from their sockets and her mouth hanging open. Oh, please. Can someone tell her this isn't a good look on her? She doesn't know he's been trying to contact me. She twirls the stem of her champagne glass between her fingers. I glance at Connor and he shrugs.

Her eyes darken and she's almost bouncing from one foot to the other. She releases the glass and watches as it falls to the floor and smashes against the ceramic tiles into a million tiny pieces.

People around us stop talking, turning to see what all the commotion is. Katherine's eyes stay on the floor; her body is shaking with anger.

"Katherine, are you okay?" Connor asks as her friend returns to see what's going on. Her friend places a hand on her shoulder, offering her some comfort, but doesn't say anything.

"No. Take your damn girlfriend away from me. She's nothing but a spiteful cunt. Why the hell would Donovan be in touch with her when he has me? She has nothing he wants!" she shouts, stepping through the glass until she's standing right in front of me. A waiter appears with a dustpan and brush to clear up the mess on the floor. He cleans up quickly without looking at any of us.

Connor attempts to take my hand, but I brush his away. I won't walk away from her. "Why don't you ask him when you see him for yourself?"

"I don't have to ask him. I trust him, and you . . . you're just the woman he left behind for me."

"Oh, please. And how long do you think he'll keep you around before he finds someone else? I'll tell you, shall I? When your money runs out." I don't shout or even raise my voice in the slightest. I'm just being honest with her; she'll realise that one day. But by then it will probably be too late.

"You really are a little bitch," she hisses, and takes a step toward me. Her friend urges her to walk away, but she refuses.

Connor steps in front of me, "Ladies, we don't need a scene."

"A scene!" she screeches in my face. "You won't get my man and I'll make sure you don't get my part. That leading part belongs to me."

"It might," I say. "And as for your man, you can keep him. I have no interest in Donovan Bell and I wish he had no interest in me."

I turn to walk away and Connor takes my hand, leading me away from the woman who seems to go out of her way to cause trouble. Although, maybe this is my fault. I shouldn't have bothered approaching her.

As I take a step away, long fingernails dig into the skin on my shoulder. I freeze and Connor's eyes widen in shock when he sees what she's doing. Guests in our vicinity have long since gone back to their own conversations. "Katherine, you have until I spin around to take your claws out of my shoulder and, if you do, nothing more will be said on the matter. Because I'm sure this incident is one you'd rather not see making headlines tomorrow."

She removes her hand and I spin around to face her. She really is a nasty piece of work. It's no wonder she's with Donovan; I'm sure the two of them are well-suited. "Katherine, I was being polite when I came over to speak to you. I really shouldn't have bothered. Good luck when it comes to the casting."

I turn on my heel and walk away. This time, Connor has his hand on the small of my back, urging me to continue walking. Neither of us turn back, but I know she'll be seething. Connor and I say goodnight to some friends and the stars of tonight's movie, who all try to talk us into going to the after party, but we respectfully decline.

My heart rate has just dropped to something that seems normal, and here I am thinking about our journey back to the hotel in the limo, which I'm sure will raise it again. Although, this time, in a good way.

"I can't make up my mind if you handled that well or not," Connor says as we reach the doorway.

There's still a few reporters and cameramen outside, hanging around, waiting to see if they get any shots that could make headline news.

"I had to go over and speak to her for myself."

"I know, and you did handle her well, although how you managed not to smack her in the mouth, I'll never know." He chuckles, opening the door, and the cold night air sends a shiver down my spine.

"Are you cold?" he asks as we wait on the car.

"A little."

"I'll heat you up."

He wraps his arms around me and pulls my body tight to his. "I'm counting on that," I say, pressing my lips to his. "We're going for a little detour."

"Oh! This sounds interesting."

Chapter 23

OUR DRIVER OPENS THE DOOR. Connor holds out his arm, indicating for me to enter first, but I need a quick word with the driver. I pause for a moment, looking at the driver and trying to avoid eye contact with Connor. *I can't ask him to take the scenic route, he'd know the reason why.* He nods his head with a smile as I enter the car and slide across the seat. I'm sure the driver knows what I'm thinking. I adjust my dress as Connor takes the seat beside me and the door closes.

The privacy glass separating us from the driver goes up.

Now our journey is about to be fun.

Connor inches his body closer to mine. I breathe him in; the scent of him instantly relaxes me as it has done these last few weeks. He takes my hand in his. "Are you okay?" he asks, and I know he's still referring to Katherine.

"I'm more than okay. I'm here with you," I say with a smile. "And we have all the time in the world."

He looks out of the window. "And what do you plan on doing with all this time we have?"

"Enjoying you. Forgetting about that mad woman I met tonight." Because that's what she is.

He reaches out and pulls me onto his lap. "Well, let's not waste it." His mouth is on mine and he's kissing me fiercely. I do what

I've wanted to do since we were in my living room at the start of our evening; I run my hands through his dark hair and kiss him back, giving myself freely to the deep passion of his kiss. There's something different about this kiss, something demanding. He's taking control and I'm happy to let him, *for the time being*.

With his hands sliding over the skin on my back, I moan. Our kiss isn't soft and gentle, it's deep and punishing, but most of all it feels needy and I can't make up my mind which of us needs it more. His grip tightens around me and he pulls me closer. I moan, this time louder than before as I feel his erection straining against my hip.

It's time to change position. He's had his small bit of control.

I tear my lips from his and he moans. I straddle him, my dress riding up my thighs. He sits before me, his eyes surveying the current situation until he smiles.

With my knees on either side of his hips and him sitting there looking as though he's just received an Oscar, I wrap my arms around his shoulder and return to kissing him. This time, I'm the one in control as I deepen the kiss. My tongue delves into his mouth, colliding with his.

Connor grabs my waist and pushes me back away from him. I frown; his eyes are narrowed and he glances around. "Ella, what are you doing to me?" he asks breathlessly.

I release my hold of him and run my hands down his chest, watching as his chest rises and falls with every breath he takes. I allow my hands to wander a little lower, tracing the fine muscles in his abdomen. He closes his eyes for a brief moment then gulps. "Me? Turning you on." I lean forward and whisper the words against his lips.

"Are you sure this is what you want? Here and now."

"Yes. I want you, here and now."

His eyes dart to the windows and I know what he's thinking, but no-one outside can see or hear us through the dark glass windows. I look out. At this time, London night life is just coming alive. Night time revellers all looking to party, and then there are those who have been out earlier in the evening, some maybe heading home. I don't think I've ever seen the streets of London deserted.

"I need you, Connor," I say breathlessly, rocking my hips against him, stroking myself against the hard length of his erection. His hissed breath through gritted teeth tells me I'm a woman who is getting exactly what she wants. "I want you."

He releases his grip on my waist and cups my face, his lips pressing hard against mine. With space still between our bodies, I lower my hands, undoing his belt and the button on his trousers and lower the zip and then his boxers. I take him in my hand and squeeze gently. He groans, the sound so damn erotic. I fist both hands around him and slide them up and down his length from root to tip.

His mouth falls away from mine and I take the opportunity to watch him as his body quivers beneath me with his eyes closed.

What a sight.

My eyes close as he reaches one hand under my dress and pushes the lace material of my thong to the side. I continue to stroke his length when I feel his fingers sliding deep inside me. He bites on his lower lip as I clench around him.

I'm desperate for more.

I reluctantly let him go and he moans. I'm not the only one missing that. Placing my hands on his shoulders to steady myself, I rise to my knees, giving myself space to hover over him. His erection brushes between my legs and I whimper. My body aches all over with need and want. I grip tighter on his shoulders to steady myself and he chuckles lightly against my ear before nibbling at my earlobe.

I drop my head to the side and he kisses my neck. Warmth floods through my veins and I can't deny the pulsing knot that has formed in my stomach. The ache between my legs grows stronger with each passing heartbeat.

I can't wait any longer. The heavy scent of our lust fills the air around us and has awakened every sense I possess.

"God, Ella." He gasps as I lower myself onto him, and his hands take a grip of my waist. Neither of us move; I'm enjoying the feel of him deep inside me.

With our eyes level and on the other, the urge to close mine is overwhelming. I wanted this intimacy. I'm the one who wanted to be in control, but as I look into the depths of his eyes, I know I'm not the one in control.

He pulls my body down harder on him, pushing himself a little deeper. I inhale deeply as my body clenches harder around him. "You're so perfect."

A brief shiver ripples through me. With our eyes still focused on the other, we start to move slowly. I want to feel every last inch of him. Our hearts beat in time with the other's. I don't see or feel him moving one hand until I feel the palm flat against my lower stomach. Everything in my core tightens when his fingers touch my clit. He teases me with expert circles, massaging me slowly.

Heavenly.

I'm fighting the heaviness in my eyes, fighting to keep them open, not wanting the connection that we're sharing to be broken, not even for a second.

Sweat beads lace his skin. He arches his neck back, head firmly against the back of the seat, yet his eyes still remain on me. "Oh God," he bites out, his teeth grinding as I slide up and down his length. "You're incredible."

He's deeper and my body is adjusting to the intrusion. Pulsing around him, I'm on the verge of an orgasm. But I want to hold back and wait for him. Tonight wasn't meant for me to be selfish. It was about me showing him that I want him; only him.

Leaning toward him, I slide my tongue along his lower lip,

at the same time lifting myself slowly from him. A tight grip on my hips pulls my body back onto him and I grab his mouth in a needy hurry as I grind against him. Kissing him hard as I rock my hips, my eyes close.

"No you don't," he says, pulling his lips from mine. I open my eyes and our connection is restored. I focus on him and on the driving urge building within me.

Connor commands the rhythm as he pulls my hips up and down. My need builds and there's no way to stop it or slow it down.

He watches me fall apart, holding my gaze. There's something erotic about him watching me grind and moan against him as I ride out my orgasm.

"Fuck . . ." he growls, thrusting his hips harder against me. I feel him tremble deep within and I watch, needing to see the moment he's pushed. His eyes darken and almost close but he regains control quickly and his eyes stay focused.

"Ella!" He cries my name as I feel him reach his own climax. His body shakes as his orgasm takes hold.

I remove my hands from his shoulders. Cupping his face, I brush my lips across his. He wraps his arms around my back, crushing my body to his. He kisses me softly. My emotions are running in all directions.

"That was incredible," he breathes against me, still looking me in the eyes. The way he's looking at me has my chest hurting. His eyes are warm and tender. "You, Ella McGregor, are full of surprises."

"I am. Our night isn't over. We still have a very inviting bed in our suite."

"We do, and I know I'll never get enough of you." I lift myself from him, sort my clothes, and sit back in the chair beside him. He wraps his arm around me and I snuggle in close to him, enjoying the comfort his body provides me with.

Who needs to go to the after party when we can have our own private party for two?

Chapter 24

"ANY MORE TEXT MESSAGES FROM Donovan?" Trevor asks as we drive through London in the back of a black cab.

"No, nothing. I thought there would be something, especially after my confrontation with Katherine last night."

"What the hell happened when I left?"

Shit! I forgot this would be news to him. He's going to be mad. I need to tell him what happened in case he has to do some sort of damage control, should Katherine have taken the story to the papers.

"I'm waiting on an explanation, Ella." Trevor is like my dad in so many ways and now is one of those times as he scowls at me, waiting for me to elaborate.

"It wasn't that bad."

"I'll be the judge of that."

I tell him everything, not leaving anything out, including the part when she insinuated that Donovan would be at the after party. I tell him that helped make up my mind on not attending.

"Okay, it doesn't sound so bad. But this is Katherine Hunter. She has a way of manipulating stories to her own advantage; just look at what happened with Alex Mathews. I'll keep a close eye and ear to the ground just in case she decides to make a song and dance out of your meeting last night." What she did to Alex was awful, accusing him of rape back in New York. But the thing that sticks in my mind is that, at the time, Libby's niece was unwell and she had to travel home to Scotland alone, not knowing what was going on with Alex.

"Thank you."

"Now, I'm going to spend much of today with you on set before I go and check out how Connor is getting on. With a bit of luck, you might get finished up early and can come with me. Are you looking forward to today?"

"Yes, I am. I love everything this company stands for. Do we know if it's the same photographer from Glasgow?"

"I'm not sure. We'll find out soon."

I turn my attention back outside and watch the world go by at an alarmingly fast pace. This is one of the reasons I love home so much; everything is so much calmer in Glasgow. What I realise as we drive is that I don't miss this fast-paced way of life. Yes, I've been enjoying the last few weeks; photo shoots, meetings with production crews, reading scripts, but I get to go home at the end of a long day. Relax and chill out. I could never do that in L.A. There was always some event or another Donovan wanted me to attend.

That lifestyle is no good for anyone. You eventually burn out.

I'm still surprised he hasn't been in touch again since yesterday. It's making me a little nervous, wondering what the hell he's playing at now.

As for him and Katherine Hunter, something isn't adding up with them. If they're together why wouldn't he attend the premiere with her?

He's playing with my mind. He's got me thinking about him and that's what he wants. Although, I'm not sure what he hopes to achieve by reaching out to me now. He should've done that months ago. Maybe it's because he realises I'm taking this further. Not only me. I know the bank is going ahead with pressing fraud charges against him.

Johnathon has been in constant contact with my dad, who has kept me up to date with everything.

"We're here," Trevor says as the cab stops. I chase my thoughts away and focus on my job. Today isn't just another job. I don't think anything I've done over the years has been *just another job*. Today is about having fun and getting the assignment done so that the client is happy with the finished product.

We exit the cab and I stand on the pavement and stare up at the building before us. I thought we were going to a studio. Instead, I find myself outside a plush hotel on the south bank of the River Thames next to Westminster Bridge. Many of the top London attractions are just a short stroll away, including the London Eye and Houses of Parliament. The view from street level is okay, but I bet the views are breath-taking from one of the many bedrooms within this historic building.

"Come on, Ella. I'm sure you'll be able to admire the views much better inside," Trevor says, pulling me from my trance-like state.

We enter, and wow. It's all high ceilings with period features, marble pillars which look original, and dark wood panel walls with lots of cream soft furnishings. Trevor leaves me gaping in this impressive and warm hotel entrance, making his way over to the reception desk. After a few minutes, he re-joins me.

"Inspire has taken over much of the hotel today. We have to go to the fitness reception where someone is waiting for us." This sounds interesting, but why would we be shooting at the gym?

We arrive at the gym and are met by Martin Brown. "Ella, wonderful to see you again," he says, kissing me on the cheek before turning and greeting Trevor. The two men exchange a few words before Martin turns back to me.

"It's great to be here," I say. "But I have to tell you now; I'm not a fitness addict."

He laughs and Trevor joins him. "That's funny. You will be modelling clothes across our whole range today, from gym gear to bathing suits, from jeans to eveningwear. I've told you before, we strive to give our customers what they want at affordable prices. Come on. You can meet everyone."

I follow behind him with Trevor at my side, and all I can think about is that I'm not sure about stripping down to a swimsuit. I'm introduced to the whole team; make-up, hair stylist, wardrobe, Will the photographer from Glasgow, and there's also a woman who introduces herself as a videographer. There's a lot of people here. Not as many as I'd find on a movie set, but a lot more than I'd expect for a photoshoot.

"Ella, don't worry. I'm staying with you as long as you need me to," Trevor says, giving me the reassurance I need.

"Can we leave the pool shots until last?" Martin calls out, asking Will the question. He nods. "Ella, can you go with make-up? Trevor, can I get you and Ella some tea or coffee?" I don't hear Trevor's response but I'm hoping he says tea as I'm led away.

The Inspire team has completely taken over the whole fitness centre; the women's changing rooms are now a dressing area, complete with everything I'd expect to see on set. There's a dressing table, and rails and rails of clothes. There's no way I'll get through all these changes today.

I do as I'm told and sit down and let everyone get on with their jobs. Make-up is applied and it looks really natural. My hair is loosely piled on my head and I'm giving my first outfit of the day to wear; casual grey jogging bottoms with a white sports bra top and trainers.

The make-up artist and hair stylist lead the way into the hotel's state of the art gym, where Will is already waiting.

"Are you ready to rock this?" Will asks as he positions me on a treadmill.

"Not if you switch this damn thing on." Everyone in the room laughs, including me.

And we start.

Moody, relaxed, and happy; these are all poses that come to me naturally today. And changing from one outfit to another so far hasn't been so demanding. "Ella, the next shot I want is you with some weights."

"You're kidding! I worked up enough sweat on the rowing machine for you."

"You did, honey, and you were fabulous. Now, here."

The squat rack. I think Will and I are about to fall out. There has been a gym instructor present the whole time. He shows me what I'm expected to do and then puts a lower weight on the bar. I stand with the bar on my shoulders, gripping it as though my life depends on it. I'm wearing a pair of shorts and a sports bra.

I feel my face flush as I think about what I have to do. "Will, are you sure you want this shot?"

"Yes."

"You only want to see my arse," I say jokingly.

"Honey, you've now given me another idea for a shot. One that includes your fine arse. Now, when I count to three, this time, I want you to squat. Don't worry if you can't lift the weight yourself. I can always edit out the instructor or keep him in. Whatever works."

He thinks I can't lift this on my own. I know I'm useless when it comes to the gym, but I want to prove him wrong. With the instructor's help, I take two steps back. "I'm fine," I say, and he lets go of the bar but stands close enough that, should there be a problem, then he can take control.

"One, two, three."

I squat down and push back up into a standing position over and over as Will snaps away, moving around me. When I rise back up after the tenth squat, Will calls out, "Cut!" The instructor takes the bar from me, telling me I did good.

"Why are you calling out cut? Are we finished?"

"I've just always wanted to say it." I shake my head at him. Bloody man. "That's us finished in the gym."

I look at the time and it's already gone three p.m. I make my way over to Trevor. "You can leave, you know? Connor needs your attention just the same as I do so you can't stay here all day."

"I know that, but . . ."

"No buts. I'm happy here with Will and the others, even though I swear he's spent longer in the gym on purpose."

"I think he has. Only if you're sure?"

"I'm sure. So go. Hopefully Connor is having more fun than me."

"What! You're not having fun, Ella?" Will interrupts my conversation. "We'll just have to make things more interesting upstairs in the function room."

"Will, take care of Ella," Trevor says, after kissing me. "If she has any complaints it's on your head."

"I promise. But why not Martin?" Will asks me. I shrug my shoulders.

My make-up is re-done, along with my hair, and I'm handed the first of many dresses and then escorted through the hotel. Will continues to take pictures as he walks behind me. He asks me to stop in the reception area and pose. I do because it's my job and I'm really enjoying it.

"WE'RE ALMOST DONE, Ella. Back downstairs to the pool and then I want to get a few shots outside with the London Eye in the background."

"Okay." It's been fun but hard work. It's now gone eight p.m. Trevor has called several times, checking up on me. He's spoken to me and Martin. There have been a few problems with Connor's filming today. Trevor wouldn't tell me what it was though, and I'm sure Connor will tell me all about it when we get back to the hotel.

Time to change *again*.

"I can't wear that!" I yell as the two-piece skimpy outfit is held before me.

"Ella, there is a range of accessories to go with it, including a sarong," Will tells me. Martin has long since gone home, along with a few others, but there's still about eight people left, not including me.

"Fine. Let's get this over with." The lady that's been dealing with my outfit changes sighs heavily, relieved. I put on the first skimpy bikini and, I have to admit, it's something I would pick for myself, I'm just not feeling confident wearing it. She hands me the sarong and we make our way to the pool area where the others are waiting. Will has already set up.

"Some pics with that but then I need some without and then I want you in the pool," he tells me. He's been very demanding today; he wasn't like this in Glasgow.

He's had me in and out of that pool for an hour and I'm at the point where I'm not sure I can smile or pose any longer.

"That's a wrap," Will calls out, and I inwardly cheer. "Ella, the ladies will take care of you."

"I thought we were finished?"

"In the pool, yes, but I want some outside shots of you all."

Ah, I remember he wanted that.

"Okay." I climb out of the pool and grab a towel.

I follow the ladies who have both been amazing today and I allow them to do their best for one last time. When they've finished, I thank them for everything. They tell me that all the outfits I've had on are now packed in a case and will return to my hotel with me along with my own clothes. Which means I'm travelling back wearing these tight ripped blue jeans and white lace top, and also the black high heels and black over-sized handbag that finishes off the outfit.

I meet Will in reception. "You look so much more relaxed now you're back in clothes," he shouts as I walk toward him. People turn and look in my direction. I want to bloody kill him. "A couple of shots on the ground then can I convince you to take a trip on the London Eye for a few more? Then I promise you we're done and the hotel will organise a taxi for you."

"Done."

"ELLA, THANK YOU so much for today. You've been incredible. And the last few shots, I think, are the best of the day. You must be tired?" he asks as we walk back to the hotel.

"Yes, I am, but I had fun too."

"Glad to hear it. Come inside the hotel and I'll organise your taxi."

"No, I'll wait out here. It's a nice night."

"Are you sure?"

"Yes, go on. I'll be fine."

He gives me the tightest of hugs and thanks me again, telling me he'll send a porter out with the case, and we part ways. I stand just in front of the entrance and wait. A porter comes out with the case and tells me the taxi won't be long and he waits with me.

The sky has darkened over the last hour, but the city is still glowing from an array of beautiful lights. The London Eye is illuminated against the skyline and bright lights shine from the many buildings around me. Terrace bars further along the bank are filled with people all enjoying their night, the start of the weekend for many.

Goosebumps spread across my skin and a deep shiver runs through me, and not in a good way. I notice a lone figure leaning against a tree across the road, watching me. There's no light behind them to show me who it is.

A taxi pulls up and the porter lifts my case and I climb in. I look through the back window as the black cab moves away and the figure steps out into the street. I still can't get a clear view of whoever it is, but in my heart I already know.

Donovan.

Chapter 25

"YOU'RE STILL REALLY FREAKED OUT!" It's not a question from Connor but a statement as we stroll through Kensington Gardens. It's dry and bright but with a slight wind bringing the temperature down. Still nice enough for a relaxing walk hand-in-hand.

"Yes. I know it was him. He was standing there just watching me. How long had he been hanging around? Had he been watching me the whole time Will was taking pictures of me outside?"

"I blame myself for Trevor being held up."

"Don't you dare. This isn't your fault. I should be able to go about my business and not have to look over my shoulder. I think his aim is to frighten me, but I'm not sure why."

"Well, I'll be with you now all the time we're here in London. And Trevor has already spoken to Johnathon to see what they can do, although he hasn't approached you in person and there's been no further messages from him."

We stop in front of the Peter Pan statue to the west of Long Water, in the same spot as Peter lands his bird-nest boat in the story, 'The Little White Bird.' The bronze statue features Peter Pan surrounded by squirrels, mice, rabbits, and fairies. It's stunning. A family nearby runs to catch up with their little girl who wants to have her picture taken beside Peter Pan. I watch on, smiling.

"You're in a world of your own."

I loved getting my picture taken when I was her age. Hopefully my own kids will be the same, if I'm lucky enough to be blessed with any. "Yes, I was. Come on. Let's finish our walk and then we should go for lunch. I'm starting to feel hungry."

"Why didn't you say?" He kisses me on my nose before pulling me along with him. Maybe I shouldn't have mentioned I was hungry because now I'm sure I won't get to enjoy our relaxing stroll through the gardens.

We pause briefly at The Albert Memorial; it is one of London's most ornate monuments. It commemorates the death of Prince Albert in 1861 of typhoid at the age of forty-two. There's lots of tourists listening to a guide telling them all about Prince Albert. It's all very interesting.

"Do you fancy anything in particular to eat?" Connor asks.

"Not really."

"I think we should walk back and head to Notting Hill. There's a beautiful Italian restaurant that I know you'll love." I nod in agreement.

We turn around and continue walking in silence. I'm trying not to dwell on last night, but it has taken me by surprise and, as Connor says, completely freaked me out. Part of me wants to get in touch with Donovan to find out what the hell he wants from me, but the sensible side tells me to stay as far away from him as I possibly can, because he's only going to bring me more trouble.

Yes, I'm curious to find out, but I'm sure Johnathon will be able to fill me in in due course. Dad was on the phone first thing this morning, checking up on me. He wanted Connor and me to come home early, but I told him no, that I wanted to enjoy our time together because when we go home, life is going to be hectic for us until we get ourselves into a routine.

Tomorrow morning, I have a meeting with the director and casting producer and Trevor, for the movie. When I read the script, it had all the feels, but one thing is putting me off. Returning to L.A.

If I get offered the part, I have plenty of time to think about it and sort myself out; filming doesn't begin for another three months.

A shiver runs through my body, much the same as it did last night. I find myself looking around us, glancing briefly over my shoulder, looking for something or *someone*. There's lots of people in the park but no one I recognise.

I'm just being foolish. This is my imagination running riot. I've never experienced feelings of being unsafe, but there's something bothering me.

Internally, I give myself a telling off.

Connor stops walking and I only notice when he pulls me roughly back, spinning me around to face him. "You really are a million miles away today," he says, a softness in his voice.

"Sorry. I have a lot on my mind."

"I know that, but you don't have to keep everything bottled up. I'm here for you. I've always been a good listener."

He pulls my body tight to his and I lean my head on his shoulder and close my eyes momentarily, accepting the comfort he's offering me. When I'm around him and things seem out of my reach, as though my life is spinning out of control, he grounds me. He doesn't usually have to say anything, just having him near or his arms around me is enough. I don't want to tell him there's a feeling of unease sweeping over me. I'm not even sure if that's what it is.

"Better?" he asks, tilting my head until I can see his bright eyes clearly.

"Yes."

"Okay." He presses his lips lightly to mine and the minute they connect, I feel the urge to deepen the kiss, but he pulls away, smirking. "No, you don't. Lunch."

"Fine." I sigh heavily.

We walk to the restaurant, although not in silence. Connor talks and it keeps my mind off everything that's going on. The restaurant sits on a corner and has outdoor seating, but I'm hoping Connor doesn't want to sit outside and watch the world go by because I'd much rather be inside. He opens the door and we step inside. It's rustic, and the smell that hits me straight away is heavenly.

I'm sure I hear my own stomach grumble and I'm not that surprised. We didn't have breakfast this morning. As soon as we were up and ready, I just wanted to go for a walk.

A waiter with a heavy Italian accent seats us in a table at the back of the restaurant, giving us an open view of the chefs at work in the kitchen. Connor orders a bottle of wine along with some water and I sit back and take in our surroundings. Wooden beam ceilings, mosaic tiles on the floor. It's perfect. We read the menu, even though I have an idea what Connor will pick. The waiter brings over our drinks and asks if we're ready to order. "Can I have Carpaccio di Manzo con Instalitina di Rucola e Parmigano to start. Followed by Gamberoni in Padella?"

"Of course; fine choice. And for you?" The waiter turns his attention to Connor.

"He'll have Ribollita alla Toscana, followed by Filleto di Vitello alla Griglia con Zucchine Croccanti. Am I correct?" I ask smugly.

"Yes," Connor says, and the waiter leaves our table, looking amused. "How do you know that?"

"We've been to enough Italian restaurants over the years for me to notice. You always pick veal if it's on the menu and, as for the soup, you've had it a few times and nothing else on the menu appealed to me for you," I say, sitting back in my chair and watching him as I take a sip of the wine that has been poured.

"You've been very observant, haven't you?"

"Yes and always. Even down to the fact that over the years

you've rarely dated and you seldom get drunk."

"I had someone in my life, and she was worth waiting for. As for getting drunk, it's not really my style." I lift my now shaky hand to my mouth and gasp. My heart swells at his words. "Ella, I can't pretend with you about how I feel. Not anymore. Not when I don't have to keep it bottled up inside. I know how I feel about you, but I'll only say those words when I know you're ready to hear them."

Tears fill my eyes, blurring my vision, but I don't want to cry. Not today. Not even with happy thoughts and feelings. He reaches across, removing my hand from my mouth, "Ella, please don't get upset. Today I just want us to relax and be happy."

"I'm trying to do both."

"I sense a but. Tell me what's wrong."

I take a deep breath. "In the park, a shiver coursed through me, just like it did last night."

"Why didn't you say anything?"

"Because I couldn't see anyone. I looked. Believe me, I looked."

"Babe, you have to talk to me. Be honest with me." I nod as the waiter comes back to our table with our starters. "Thank you," we say at the same time. The waiter nods before leaving us.

Silence fills the air around us and I don't like it. He's frustrated with me and I can't blame him. It's going to be hard sharing thoughts and feelings. I've always made decisions on my own.

I was the one feeling uneasy and I was the one who made the decision not to tell him my thoughts and fears. Which is silly, given the fact I was able to tell him about last night.

What's the difference?

Is it because today it's bright, and last night it was dark and I was tired?

"Connor, I'm sorry. I should've mentioned it, especially given how I'm feeling," I say, desperate to change the atmosphere that has built up between us. I don't want to argue or fall out with him.

"I know you are. But you frustrate me. All I want to do is be here for you and with you."

"So I'm forgiven?"

"Of course. Now, tomorrow's meeting. Are you ready for it?" he asks, and the subject is changed and normal conversation resumes.

I tell him my fears. The *what if I get offered the part*? Connor tells me that if I do get the part and need to be in L.A, he'll be there with me. I can't help but smile as he reinforces the words he's told me before.

The rest of our lunch passes without further event, and when we leave, I'm happier and more relaxed than I have been all day.

I stop on the pavement outside the restaurant and face him, taking his hand in mine. He wraps his other arm around my back and softly presses his mouth against mine. Unlike earlier, I have no desire to rush or take more from this kiss. This kiss is everything I want and need right now. Slow and thoughtful, just like the man before me.

"Where to now?" he asks.

"The hotel."

"No. How about we go shopping?"

Chapter 26

SHOPPING. I THOUGHT HE WAS kidding, but here we are in Bond Street; an exclusive shopping area in London. I wanted to keep a low profile but there's no chance of doing that here. This is where people come to be seen.

"Ella, what's wrong?" Connor asks, frowning at me.

"I'd have been happy mooching around a market today."

"Babe, please humour me."

I nod unconvincingly. I don't want to be in and out of all these expensive shops, and I certainly won't be buying anything, especially when money can be better spent elsewhere. He grabs my hand and we stroll along the street. The street is lined with some, if not the best designer shops in the world including Prada, Ralph Lauren, Chanel, and Louis Vuitton.

Relief fills me as we pass some of the exclusive designer stores. It's funny how my attitude has changed recently; it wasn't that long ago that these stores were where I would shop. Over the years, Julie and I would have girlie shopping weekends here in London. I never thought twice about the amount of money I would spend on clothes, or anything else, for that matter. Now, though, my attitude is changing.

I'm looking forward to my meeting during the week with the charity that Trevor has put me in touch with. It will be good to learn all about their aims and hear what help and assistance they need. Dad is coming with me because he wants to help too, and I'm more than happy to work alongside my dad to raise awareness and much needed funds for the charity.

Connor stops. "Come on, we're going in here," he says, standing outside Tiffany. The doorman smiles as he says, "Good afternoon," before opening the door. I've been in this store a few times with my dad, who has very good taste when it comes to buying jewellery. The question on the tip of my lips is: why are we here?

An elegant lady walks toward us as soon as we enter. There's not a strand of her hair out of place; she has the whole Audrey Hepburn look going on and pulls it off beautifully. "Afternoon. How can I help you today?" she asks looking at me, then at Connor. After a moment, she smiles, recognising us.

"Hi," I reply with a smile. That's all I can say because I don't know why we're here.

"Afternoon," Connor finally says. "I do hope you can help me. I'm looking for something almost as beautiful as the woman beside me."

"Anything in particular?" she asks, her perfect smile in place.

"Yes. No." The woman walks toward one of the glass displays with Connor, both deep in conversation. I stay rooted to the spot, watching him. He turns back, expecting me to have moved, but I can't. "Ella, what's wrong?" He rushes back to me.

"Why are we here?"

"Because I want to treat you. You deserve to be spoiled and I plan on doing that. I wanted to get you a surprise but then thought it would be nice to do this together. So here we are."

I'm a bit taken aback. The only men who have ever bought me jewellery are my dad and Callum. In five years together, Donovan never bought me so much as a pair of earrings. "Come on. I have an idea of what I'd like to get but I want to make sure you like it too. No arguments, either. I know what you're like." He takes my hand, gently pulling me toward the assistant.

We're in front of a stunning bracelet display. The woman has already taken a few items out and has them on the glass counter before us. "Madam, do you have a preference? A cuff or a full bracelet?"

"Please, call me Ella, and no preference."

"Okay, Ella. May I?" she asks, reaching for my hand and proceeding to turn my hand over and study my wrist. "I personally think a cuff, but you are more than welcome to try on both types." I glance down at my wrist and wonder if she's making that up.

I glance at the bracelets; none come with a price tag, which usually wouldn't bother me, but after everything, I'm not happy with Connor wanting to spend lots of money on me. Especially when, these days, I wouldn't spend it on myself.

This is getting ridiculous. I need to put the past behind me and move on and not feel guilty about spending money.

"Ella . . ."

I turn to Connor. "Sorry. I was a million miles away."

"It's fine. If you can't pick, I will."

"You pick."

I watch him pick up several bracelets and look them over before putting them all back down. "Can we try this one?" He picks up a gorgeous white gold and diamond cuff.

"Of course." The assistant gently puts it on my wrist, smiling proudly when she stands back, allowing Connor and me to admire it. It is exquisite. "The Tiffany Infinity is a powerful symbol of continuous connection, energy, and vitality. The round diamonds add a heightened level of impact to this already striking design. It's 18k white gold and the Carat weight is .39," she tells us.

When I look at Connor, his eyes are sparkling with happiness; this is the one he wants to buy. It's gorgeous and I love it. "We'll take it," Connor says softly, looking at me. I nod with a smile.

"Perfect. Let me box it for you." I wander around the store, looking at all the stunning pieces of jewellery, leaving Connor with the assistant. I can hear them talking but don't pay attention.

"Are you ready?" Connor asks, slipping one hand into mine and handing me the bag in the other.

"Yes, and thank you. Not just for this, or today, but for just being you and being here for me. For reminding me of the person I was."

"You don't have to say thank you to me ever, but . . ." He presses his lips to mine. "You are more than welcome to show your gratitude when we're back at the hotel," he whispers. Shivers lace my back at his words. Words I'll gladly take him up on.

We say goodbye and leave the store. It's only about a ten-minute walk from here to our hotel in Piccadilly and it's still a nice afternoon. We've covered more than a few miles today, but it's been relaxing. Nothing about today has been rushed. I'm glad we didn't make any firm plans to do anything. A show would've been nice but I've enjoyed the time we've spent together and now I'm looking forward to our evening.

We walk in silence, still hand-in-hand, offering each other a warm smile when we get caught glancing at the other. Each time I look his way, I see something else I like in the man I'm spending more and more of my time with.

We're almost at the hotel; I can see the flags above the main entrance and the doorman standing outside talking to someone, when cold shivers run down my spine. My racing heart feels as though it could explode at any moment. I freeze and close my eyes. My body shakes.

"Ella. Ella, what's wrong?" I hear Connor's voice and I know he's standing in front of me, gripping onto my shoulders, but as I open my eyes, I don't see him. I don't see anything, but I sense there's someone watching me again. I search around and behind us, but still see nothing, or no-one. "Ella, talk to me. Shit, you're pale."

"He's here, somewhere. I can feel him." The words leave me in a whispered rush. The hazy cloud that was blurring my vision leaves me and I see the panic on Connor's face as he watches me.

He looks around us, searching, "Ella, there's no-one here. He's not here. Come on. Let's get into the hotel."

I try to move my legs but they're not working. I'm dizzy and my legs are weak. Everything around us is moving by too quickly and I can't process what's happening to me. Images of Donovan flash through my mind. *He's standing behind me, laughing at my inability to run.* All I see is black spots before me. My body sways and I can't stop it from sinking. The weight is pulling me down. I try to take in a deep breath, but there's no oxygen for me to breathe. There's nothing. Only darkness.

"No, you don't. I have you."

He lifts me into his arms as though I'm weightless. I bury my face into his chest, wanting to hide myself from any onlookers who may have noticed my panic attack in the middle of a street in London. Voices I don't know are around us, asking if everything is okay, asking Connor if he needs help. Pain consumes my entire body as he walks briskly toward the hotel.

"Mr Andrews, can I help?" I open my eyes and see the concerned look of the doorman. *I don't need anyone to see me like this.*

"I only need help with the lifts."

"Of course." Silence fills the air until I hear the ping of the lift. Footsteps ring loudly in my ears and hushed voices speak around me. I sense the movement of the lift and my body wriggles in Connor's hold. I want him to let me go. I don't want him or anyone to see me right now.

Pushing my hands against his chest, I attempt to wriggle from his hold, but he only grips onto me tighter.

A door opens and lights are switched on. I open my eyes to see we're in our suite. Connor still has me in his arms and walks toward the bedroom. He gently lowers me to the bed and I close my eyes because we're not alone in the room. "Please, I want to be on my own," I whimper, turning my back to even Connor.

"Sorry, Ella. I'm not going anywhere."

"Mr Andrews, I think we should get a doctor for the cut on her hand. It looks as though there's something in it."

"Can you arrange for a doctor to come here?"

"Consider it done." I hear heavy footsteps crossing the carpeted floor.

"Ella, it's only you and me now. Talk to me, please. I can't help or understand if you don't explain."

I turn over and lie on my back. His eyes are sad; he's clearly unsettled by what's happening. "That wasn't the first time I've felt strange, as though someone's watching me. I know you must think I'm crazy, but honestly, I'm not. I know he was near."

"I believe you," he says, stroking the side of my face. His attention soon turns to my hand. "It does look as though there's something in this cut. Maybe just a small stone." My eyes follow his and he might be right. I should get up and attempt to clean it.

My phone buzzing has me scanning the room for my handbag. Connor bends down and picks it up from the floor. He takes my phone and stares at the screen, his eyes wide, looking in disbelief. I already know it's either a call or message from Donovan.

"Tell me?"

"He's sent some pictures of today. A few from Kensington Park, the restaurant, and from outside in the street."

I grab my phone from his hands and swipe through each of the pictures. My lips tremble and I can't form any words. What is he hoping to achieve from this? My hand shakes as I get to the last picture; me in Connor's arms as he carries me back to the safety of our hotel.

But is our hotel safe? Why do I feel as though I'm being punished? I've not done anything wrong. Or have I?

"Trevor, can you come to the hotel? . . . We have a

problem . . . Donovan fucking Bell." I look at Connor through my tear-filled eyes. "I'll forward you what Ella has been sent."

My phone beeps in my hand and I open the message from Donovan. No pictures, only his words.

Not so strong now. I've been keeping my eye on you and will continue to do so. You don't belong to him.

You have and will always belong to me.

Connor snatches the phone from my hands and reads the message. "Ella, he's playing games. He can't hurt you," he says, joining me on the bed and wrapping his arms protectively around me, but I'm not feeling safe and his words aren't helping my growing fears.

Donovan is going to do whatever he can to hurt me and that alone frightens me.

Chapter 27

"ARE YOU GLAD TO BE home?" Connor asks as we enter my house and I switch off the alarm.

"Yes. I've had a great time with you." I spin around to face him in the hallway. "But I had forgotten how tiring it can get. And then there's all the other stuff." Donovan played heavily on my mind as we travelled home. Neither of us has heard from him since his last text message yesterday. I know he's playing games and trying to upset me, and I've let him. So he'll now be thinking he's winning.

Today is a new day, and I'm trying to put on a brave face.

"I know what you mean." He lifts my right hand and studies the white gold and diamond bracelet that he insisted on buying me yesterday when we went shopping. Not only did he buy the bracelet, but there was another gift box in the bag when I opened it last night. Diamond stud earrings, and they are beautiful. We had a small disagreement about them which took my mind off another man, if only for a short time. "It suits you."

"I love it, and the earrings. Thank you."

"You don't have to keep saying thank you, but I'll happily sit back and allow you to show your appreciation later, if you feel up to it," he teases. Donovan managed to ruin what plans I had for our evening together. I'm sure we were both looking forward to a cosy evening last night.

"Oh, I don't know if I feel up to it," I tease. "I'm sure your wait will be worth it."

"Spoil sport." I pick up the mail that's lying on the sideboard; my dad must have been here over the weekend, or maybe it was Callum. As I turn my back to him, Connor playfully slaps my arse. I'm not even going to respond. Leaving him laughing in the hallway, I flick through the mail as I walk through to the kitchen. There doesn't look to be anything too important, although . . .

My fingers shake and I freeze in the middle of the kitchen, dropping all the letters on the floor as though I've just burnt my hand. I stare at the pile and I see it clearly. The writing stares back at me. I would know it anywhere.

"Will we just order a takeaway for dinner? It's been too long a day and I know I don't want to start cook . . ." Connor stops talking as he bangs into me. "What is it? What's wrong?" His eyes dart from me to the floor and he gets it. "Oh, for fuck's sake! What is wrong with him?"

He takes his phone from his pocket and makes a call. He paces anxiously from one foot to the other, waiting for someone to answer. "Donovan, call me. We need to talk," he finally says when I presume the call goes to voicemail.

"What the hell were you going to say to him if he answered?" I shout at him, confused.

"I don't know, but I can't stand back and watch him torment you at any chance he gets, because that's what he's doing." He steps toward me, ignoring the mess of letters on the floor. "Ella, you can't let him win."

"Can you call Trevor and my dad? I'm going to have a shower," I say, walking away from him.

"Ella," he calls after me, but I don't turn back. I don't mean to be distant or hurt him, I'm just trying to give myself a bit of space, a few minutes to myself. To clear my mind. To rid my head of all thoughts of Donovan Bell because I know he's trying to drag me back down. But I'm not letting him. I need to sort this mess out once and for all.

Ensure he stays out of my life.

I'M DISAPPOINTED CONNOR didn't come up the stairs, but I get that he's probably giving me the space I so desperately need. Time alone with my thoughts, to sort my head out. I've been upstairs longer than I had planned, but I think I'm in a better frame of mind now than I was earlier. I hear everyone's voices as I near the bottom of the staircase; Trevor, my dad, Callum, and Connor.

Connor is the only person standing as I enter the kitchen and pause; the others are all sat around the island. Connor turns, facing me, and crosses the short space between us. I wrap my arms around his neck. "I'm sorry," I say.

"It's fine," he says, rubbing my back and holding me tightly. I could stay in his arms forever. "Are you ready to talk?"

"Yes." He keeps one arm around me and we walk over to the others, who are all watching us. Connor pulls a chair out and releases his hold of me and I sit down. The letter that I dropped from Donovan lies before me. "Have you opened it?" I ask.

"No. Sweetheart, are you okay?" my dad asks, sounding worried.

"Does she look okay?" Callum shouts. And I thought I looked better; obviously not.

"Callum!"

"I'm okay, all things considered. It's been a tough weekend."

"It sounds like it. Trevor and Connor have been keeping me up to date on everything. We have a lot to discuss."

I pick up the letter. Connor places his hands on my shoulders, offering me comfort. I smile up at him and draw strength from him, and slowly I open the envelope. I take a deep breath before

I read it out.

Dear Ella,

This is the only way I can communicate with you, although I'm not even sure you'll read it. This could be a complete waste of my time.

We need to talk. I need to see you face-to-face. Alone, just me and you, without interruptions. I know I've fucked up but I want the chance to put this right. I need you as much as you need me. Please call me.

I love you.

Donovan

"Is that it?" Callum asks, scraping his chair across the kitchen floor and walking over to the sink. He stands, his arms outstretched, leaning against the work surface and looking out of the window.

"That's it."

"Ella." It's Trevor's voice I turn back to as Connor still holds me. "I've seen the messages and pictures Donovan has sent you and I can only advise you that you have to take this further and not have any contact with him."

"Trevor is right. As much as I want nothing more than to come face-to-face with him and smack him in the mouth, I'm not willing to put you in harm's way. Donovan has gone to a lot of effort over the weekend to follow your movements and frighten you. I think it's time to take this further, sweetheart. We need to call the police. We also need to keep tabs on him, find out where he is," Dad says softly, and I know he wants to have someone look into his whereabouts. Have them follow him.

Connor kneels down in front of me and clears his throat, but his eyes look sad. He reaches out, taking my hands in his, softly stroking his fingers along mine. "Ella, we don't know what he's capable of. We all want to keep you safe."

I look around my family and see the same look on each of their faces; a mixture of sadness and frustration. "Ella, here's how it's going to play out." Callum's deep voice echoes around the room. "You are going to do what you're told for once. The police will be called. Dad will instruct Jonathon to do whatever he needs to do to find that piece of scum, and until we know what the hell he's playing at, you won't go anywhere alone."

"Hold on," I protest, my voice raised. "You can't tell me what I can and can't do."

"I can, and you'll find we're all in agreement about this," Callum tells me at the same time Connor's phone buzzes. He stands, taking it from his pocket, and reads the message he's been sent.

A sour taste fills my mouth and there's a deep ache in the back of my throat as I look at Connor. He glares at his phone, nostrils flared, a slight reddening of his face. He drops his phone on the work surface before kneeling back before me. "Ella, we only want you to be safe and happy. I want you to be happy." He's holding something back.

Callum lifts Connor's phone and reads the message out loud. "You finally have what you've always wanted, but not for long. You can never make her truly happy. She's not yours to keep."

"I don't belong to anyone, and especially not him." I stand, pushing Connor's hands away, and walk away from the four of them. Opening the patio doors, I go outside. It's starting to get dark and cold. The trees in the garden sway in the wind that seems to be picking up. I wrap my arms around me. I was so confident after my shower that I was going to deal with this head on, arrange to meet with Donovan if I have to, to ensure he stays away from me. What is it he wants from me?

He doesn't love me. Or want me in his life. If he did, he wouldn't have done all the things he's done to me, starting with the affair he had two years ago. Part of me wishes I didn't know about that now. It's just something else for me to feel angry about, and I don't want to feel angry anymore.

I just want to be happy and get on with my life without Donovan Bell popping up and playing his fucking mind games.

"Hey, sis."

I turn, hearing Callum's soft voice. "Did you get the short straw?" I ask as he wraps his arm around me, and I rest my head on his shoulder.

"Something like that. Talk to me. What are you thinking?"

"I don't know anymore. Earlier, I was feeling confident I wasn't going to let his games affect me, because I know what he's doing. We all do. But, if I'm honest, I'm scared. I never thought he'd stoop to following me and taking pictures, sending me message after message, and now he's sending messages to Connor. Who will it be next?"

"Ella, you haven't done anything wrong and it's okay to be scared. But I'd never let Donovan hurt you."

"He already has."

"You have to let us help."

"Help in what way? I'm sure Dad will organise a private investigator, but then what?"

"Then you take out an injunction against him. That means he'll be breaking the law if he continues to hound you."

"Maybe."

"There's no maybe about it. You need him out of your life so you can move forward. Donovan is doing this because he's lost clients in recent weeks, ever since you spoke out. People don't want to work with him, and who can blame them when they think he's going to swindle money from them."

This is news to me.

"Here's the thing. Your story made news here in the UK, but in the States, it's *still* making news. Regardless of what you think about yourself as far as the industry is concerned, you are still one of the best actresses in the world at the moment."

Tears fall slowly down my face at his words, because it all hits home. Self-doubt has been a big thing for me in recent months. I thought I was over all this and putting it behind me, but I've not, not really. I love my career, but everything with Donovan has left me thinking I wasn't good enough for him; that I had done something wrong. I believed that was why he did what he did.

But Callum is right. Of course my situation was going to make headlines, especially in the States, where he's based. It's upsetting me to think that in the months leading up to the day Donovan left, I thought I wasn't good enough in the industry because there had been no recent job offers.

"Hey, it's okay to cry. But you can't allow him to control your life."

"I know that, but . . ."

"Let Dad sort this, and as for Connor, you let that man into your heart. He's hurting too because he feels useless. He wants to be there for you. To protect you. But I can see it, you're already starting to push him away and that's not fair. Do you know I've waited years for you to pick the right man? A man that loves you for who you are, not what you're worth."

"Okay. I'll let Dad do what he has to do, and as for Connor, I promise I'll try not push him away."

"Good girl. Let's go and tell them. We can call the police, and while we wait for them, you can tell us all about yesterday's casting audition. Because I've already heard through the grapevine that they haven't called Miss Hunter for hers after her stunt at the premiere."

I smile smugly and walk back inside with my brother who, for once in his life, seems to be talking sense.

When did he get all grown up and wise?

Chapter 28

IT'S FOUR A.M. AND I'VE tossed and turned since I came to bed a few hours ago. Donovan has been at the forefront of my mind and I didn't want to fall asleep thinking about him because, in the past, that's only lead to a troubled sleep and nightmares.

And I had nightmares about him for long enough. I don't want to go back to the darkness and crying that consumed me night after night when I first found out what a mess he'd left me with. I know I'm better than that, but here I am, allowing him to have undeniable control over my life.

I should get up because, if I lie here much longer, I'm going to wake Connor and that's not fair on him. So far, he's been understanding considering all I've wanted to do is push him away. And why have I been pushing him away? Because, in my head, if I push him away now, then it won't hurt as much as it would months down the line when he decides I'm not worth the pain and trouble. I'm struggling to understand what he sees in me. I don't get it. With me, there comes so much baggage.

Pushing the bed covers from my body, I swing my legs off the bed.

"Where do you think you're going?" he asks. I thought he was still sleeping.

"I didn't want to disturb you."

"So you thought it would be better sneaking out of my bed in the middle of the night? Ella, sneaking about and hiding doesn't suit you. Come on. Back into bed and talk to me."

We do need to talk, or rather I need to talk to him, not shut him out. I need to be honest with him.

He pulls me right beside him and I rest my head on his bare chest. The steady rhythm of his breathing is soothing at the best of times, but there's something more. There's a connection between us, and in moments like this, he makes me feel calm and want to stay with him forever.

Forever. Is that really what I want? I don't know. I'm not even sure how I feel about us, about him. My thoughts are a jumbled mess, and until my life is back to some sort of normality, I can't think about what my feelings are for him.

"Ella, please. I can't help if you won't talk to me."

"I'm not being fair on you. There's too much going on in my life to even think about you. Us."

"Okay." I hear the pang of sadness in his voice. "But at least you've acknowledged there is an us. Ella, I promised you I wouldn't push you into anything you didn't want to do. I told you we'd slow things down but you didn't want that. I've given you control. Everything that's happened between us is because it's what you wanted. I can't deny my feelings for you, and if you decide you want to go back to being friends, then we will. Because I love you enough to give you the space you need." I lift my head. "Stay where you are. I don't want to see sadness and regrets in your eyes. And I certainly don't want the words said to me out of guilt, but for me, there'll never be anyone else I could ever love. You've been it for me since our very first meeting five years ago. You deserve to be treated with respect and, in my opinion, that's how he should've treated you. I can't change the past, but if you allow me, I can shape our future."

He runs his fingers through my hair as I wipe my eyes. I'm

not going to cry but that has to be the nicest thing anyone has ever said to me.

"I've been scared to close my eyes and fall asleep because I don't want to have nightmares about him," I say as he comforts me.

"And you think that's what's going to happen?" I nod against his warm skin. "If it did, I'd be right here beside you to hold you."

"I know that, and that scares me too."

"I don't understand."

"I don't want to confuse my feelings for you. I don't want to become dependent on you to help me through bad times. If everything works out for us, it has to be because we both want it."

He kisses me on the head and I know he understands what I'm trying to say, even though I'm struggling to say the words. "Let's try and get some sleep."

"Okay."

"YOU LOOK GORGEOUS," says Connor as I enter the kitchen. He doesn't look so bad himself considering neither of us got a great amount of sleep. He stands there in a pair of worn jeans and a white shirt that's turned up at the sleeves. His hair is messy perfection and I wouldn't have it any other way. "Are you ready for today?"

"Yes. I'm looking forward to this. What about you?"

"Of course I am. I'm spending more time with a beautiful woman and I'm finding out all about the charity you want to help. What more could a man want?" I blush and smooth down my cream dress, thinking maybe I'm a bit over-dressed for today's meeting now that I see him.

I walk towards him as he leans against the sink. "Thank you and sorry," I say, pressing my lips to his. "And I'm glad you'll be there today."

"Well, I do have to keep an eye on you and make sure you're okay."

"I'm sure between you and my dear dad today, I won't get a minute on my own."

"As it should be. How are you feeling?"

"I'm actually really good and I've come to a few decisions."

He wraps his arms around my waist, pulling me closer to him. "And what are those?"

"Firstly, Trevor has emailed. I've been offered the part in the movie. Filming doesn't start for a few months and it's being shot between L.A and London."

He smiles at me. He already knows what I'm going to say. "You're accepting then?"

"Yes. I'd be foolish not to, especially when I already know the producers here in Scotland are prepared to work around my schedule. I'm not going to allow Donovan to hold me back from doing the job I'm passionate about."

"Glad to hear it. You need this, just as I need . . ." He stops talking, not wanting to finish what he was saying, but he doesn't have to. *You*. The single word he hasn't said hangs in the air between us. He needs me.

And I'm starting to realise I need him too, but I want him more. My thoughts on every part of my life are mixed up, but I know for sure that my feelings for Connor Andrews are deepening with each passing day. Yet, still I feel confused.

"Stop thinking and just kiss me already."

"Pretty sure of yourself, aren't you?"

"Of course, and why shouldn't I be? You've already seen all I have to offer."

I stifle a laugh. "I've seen your package." I cover my mouth with my hand in both embarrassment and amusement. He laughs and I'm sure my face is red.

"Yes, and I've had no complaints," he says, leaning his head forward. His mouth is as close as it can be without touching.

"No complaints, huh? I'm sure I can find something to complain about."

"I bet you can't. You have bagged yourself some hot property, if I do say so myself."

Oh, please. I grab his face, pulling his lips to mine, and cover his mouth, silencing him before he speaks again. His tongue traces the soft fullness of my lips before reclaiming them, crushing his mouth to mine, more demanding than before. I melt against not just his kiss, but his body.

I'm home.

I'm where I belong.

And the funny thing is, my thoughts don't frighten me.

"Babe, we need to go or we'll be late. And as much as I'm loving this kiss, I don't want to be the one to ruin your plans." His voice whispers against my lips as he pulls back from me, leaving me longing for more.

"YOU LOOK SO much better than you did last night," my dad says, embracing me as soon as we exit my car.

"I'm feeling better. Honestly," I tell him. It was late by the time everyone left. I felt as though the police officers were at my house for hours questioning me. God, at one point I even thought I was the criminal.

"Okay, then let's get inside and see what we're dealing with. After this, meeting we'll go for lunch and I'll tell you how things went with Jonathon." I had forgotten, or conveniently pushed to the back of my mind, that Dad was meeting with our lawyer this morning about Donovan.

Turning my concentration to now, the three of us walk toward the building, ready and eager to find out what we can do to help the charity.

"Good afternoon, Miss McGregor. It's lovely to finally meet you. I'm Michelle." The woman before me shakes my hand.

"Please, just Ella. This is my dad, Archie, and this is Connor."

"Pleased to meet you. Let's go to my office and I can tell you all about our charity and then you can meet some of the staff and volunteers who regularly help out at shelters across the city and on the streets at night."

A shiver runs through me with her last words and my thoughts drift back to the man from a few weeks ago, wondering how he is. Did he get the job he was going for? I hope so.

We sit down in her office and wait for her to start talking.

"We are a charity organisation that works to alleviate the distress caused by homelessness and bad housing. We do this by giving advice, information, and advocacy to people in housing need, and by campaigning to end the housing crisis our country faces for good. As a charity, we can't provide homes, but we can provide all the help and support people need with housing problems. We are the lifeline some people need in order to get their lives back on track."

"We also work alongside local councils and social care departments, and other charity organisations. I can show you our reports and achievements and tell you what we hope to achieve this year."

"So I can clarify, you help not just those on the streets, but those who find themselves in poor accommodation?" Dad asks.

"Yes, and you'd be surprised at how bad some conditions are. I'm personally working alongside a young mum with two young girls who, through no fault of their own, lost everything after her partner died. Some of the stories are tragic."

We spend over an hour talking in her office, hearing about everything the charity does. From helping with housing issues, to finding a homeless person a bed for a night in a shelter, which we're told there aren't enough of, to providing hot food and drinks, to providing men and women on the streets with basic everyday essentials. All the things I take for granted. It's heart-breaking to hear.

In today's society, people shouldn't be living on the streets, relying on hand-outs from passers-by. We meet some volunteers who are getting organised to go to local soup kitchens where they can provide hot meals and advice, should anyone want it. We learn that the local authority is working with the charity and opens up some community centres that would be closed at night.

The advice and information given is different to each individual, but can include help with jobs, housing, benefits, and even advice for alcoholics and drug users.

We're back in Michelle's office, talking about a TV campaign she would like me to front, and I have no hesitation in backing this. I wanted to help before I came here today, but now, after hearing all the stories, I want to help more than ever.

"Michelle, I'd like to make a donation today," my dad says, taking her by surprise.

"Oh, okay," she says flustered. "I'm sure we can organise this."

"You'll have to provide me with details so I can arrange with my bank manager." The minute he says that, I look at him and he smiles. "I'd like to boost your funds by giving you a sizable amount of money."

"Erm, I don't know what to say."

"You don't have to say anything. The facts you're telling us are almost unbelievable. To think that in this day and age we still can't combat the homeless issue. I'm hoping my donation of five hundred thousand will help."

"Wow, bloody hell. All my professionalism has just left me." I laugh at her honest evaluation of herself. Trust my dad. "Archie, that is very kind. I can't wait to report back to the board about this."

"Michelle, I understand you have to report to the board, but I'd appreciate it if my name stays out of the media. As far as anyone else is concerned, this will be an anonymous donation."

"If that is your wish, of course. But I'd love to be able to keep you updated on where and who it helps the most."

Our meeting continues and we discuss the advertising campaign the company wants me to head, and I'm more than happy to do so, but it doesn't seem enough. "Michelle, I'd also like to offer my services for anything I can help with."

"Ella, you are already doing enough. Just having your name linked with us will bring in more money to help more people."

"Yes, I know, but I'd like to help."

"We never turn volunteers away so we happily accept. I understand you'll have a busy schedule, but I'm more than happy to give you more details."

"Yes, please." After discussing finer details for the advertisement I'm to be a part of, we leave Michelle after she thanks us all for today.

"Well, that went well, don't you think?" Dad asks as we stand in the car park.

"Yes, it did." Today went better than expected and I'm pleased to be able to do my bit for a charity that helps so many.

"Now that I've made Michelle's day, let's get to the restaurant and I'll make your day too, by telling you all about my meeting with Jonathon." He gets in his own car after telling us which restaurant to meet him at.

"Archie McGregor is full of surprises," Connor says, sliding into the driver's seat of my car.

"Yes, he is." What he did was something my mum would've done had she been here.

Chapter 29

THE LAST FEW DAYS HAVE been quiet concerning Donovan. There's been no contact from him and I'm glad. Jonathon found out he's still in the UK; he's staying at the Savoy in London. How can a man who is broke pay for fancy hotels? I can only presume his new girlfriend is paying for it, because Katherine Hunter is still in the UK too. I took out an injunction against him, and I'm glad because if he does get in touch or attempt to come near me, then the police can do something about it.

It's given me some sort of peace of mind.

After Callum told me that my story was very much in the news across the Atlantic, I did some digging and called a few friends. It would seem Donovan hasn't been the first to abuse his position. But no one else has come out and made an allegation of fraud or anything else for that matter. There are lots of rumours flying around Hollywood, except my story; that's the truth.

One of the chat shows in L.A. wants to do a live interview with me. I told them I'm more than happy to but I won't be back in the States for a few months when filming starts. They said they were happy to do a live link to talk through what Donovan did to me. The chat show host wants everyone to know so, as she said, no-one else falls victim to him.

Julie was here last night for dinner and a catch-up. She's just getting over the cold, but I was missing her. Connor didn't come home until late; he'd been in meetings all day with Trevor, so Julie and I had a few drinks, a takeaway, and plenty of laughs.

She commented more than once about how relaxed I seemed. And she's right; I am more relaxed. The last few days have shown me who I should be. I can have days or moments when I'm weak, as long as my strength shines through, and it has.

It's Friday evening and Connor has called to say he's on his way home. I'm desperate to see him. He left before eight this morning and today has been the first day this week where I've had nowhere to go. I've done absolutely nothing except read. Well, that's not true; I've showered and put on clean PJs. I used to read a lot, but over the last few years there's always been something or someone to stop me.

The noise of my car stopping in the drive outside has my attention. Connor has been saying for the last few days he'll need to get his own car, but I told him at the moment he doesn't need to. There are two cars in my drive; one usually sits doing nothing for months.

"Honey, I'm home," he calls out, making me giggle and lift my head from my book. "Where are you?"

"I'm in the front room."

"Have you even got dressed today?" he asks, looking at me lying on the couch.

"Yes. I even had a shower." He laughs. "What's wrong?" I ask with concern as I finally take in his tired appearance.

"I've got a bit of a sore head and throat."

I sit up and put my book down and he joins me on the couch. "Do you need me to do anything for you?"

"I can think of one or two things," he says, grinning. "I'm sure that would make me feel better."

"I'm not so sure. Maybe you should go to bed on your own and get plenty of rest." He pushes me back down on the couch and starts tickling me. "Stop," I cry out.

"No," he laughs, winking at me. "You seem to be enjoying it."

I throw my arms around him, wrapping him in a tight embrace in the hope he stops his ongoing tickling assault. I feel as though I've waited all day to see him and, now that he's here on top of me, I want him.

"Please, Connor. Stop, I can't take any more."

He finally stops, but keeps me in his arms. "I've missed you," he whispers against my lips. Lips that are now desperate for his touch. We spend what seems like minutes gazing into each other's eyes before his lips finally fall to mine.

I'm where I want to be, in the arms of my sexy man with his mouth on mine. Yes, I'm in heaven.

I moan, running my hands through his hair as we deepen the kiss. Tongues dance, lapping and circling slowly. This kiss is full of the dreamy intimacy I was reading about in my book, the kind of kiss every woman should have at least once in their lives. I've felt like this with every kiss we've shared.

Releasing my mouth, he sits back on his heels, leaving me hot and bothered and craving more. He looks down through his hooded eyes; I can still see he looks tired but he's decided that this is more important than sleep. He's deep in thought and I wish I knew what he was thinking.

He lifts my pyjama top, pulls it over my head, and discards it on the floor. A warm hand cups my breast and my eyes fall closed as he pays special attention to it. The gentle massage sends currents of desire through me. He rubs my nipple between his fingers and I moan softly from the warm sensation that floods through my veins before turning his attention to my other breast and repeating his actions. His touch is light and teasing.

My body writhes beneath him from his touch. I open my eyes and he's watching me intently, his lips still moist from our kiss. He removes his t-shirt, pulling it over his head and throwing it down on the floor beside mine and then loosens the buttons on his jeans.

Where the hell is he going? I almost whimper as he stands up and I watch as he kicks off his shoes. Slowly, he lowers the jeans and his boxers before removing them completely, allowing me a moment to worship my man. I clench my legs together to alleviate the building tension. There's no doubt he's a fine specimen of a man as he stands before me, completely naked.

Connor takes a step toward me and lowers his hands, finding the waistband of my shorts before quickly removing them and they join the pile of discarded clothes on the floor.

He crawls slowly back on the couch, parting my legs, exploring my thighs then moving slowly up. My eyes close when he runs his tongue along my clit. I cry out when he plunges his tongue deep inside me before pulling out and doing it again.

Dear God.

His hands reach out, grabbing my hips, trying to hold me in place, but it's no use. My hips are rotating to meet him, seeking further friction. Wanting more. He lifts his mouth and all I feel is cool air where I want to feel him. I know if I open my eyes, I'm going to see him staring at me with amusement on his face as I wait impatiently on him returning to the torturous pleasurable task in hand.

I don't open my eyes; I silently pray that he continues.

And he does, increasing the pressure. I grab onto the couch and push my hips closer to him. My body begins to vibrate with liquid fire as the intensity builds, heating through my body. I arch my back, needing more pressure, more him, more everything. His tongue leaves me briefly before plunging deep back into me. Gusts of desire flood through me. I explode around him and an uncontrollable joy fills me.

Opening my eyes, I see a satisfied Connor Andrews staring lovingly up at me. He kisses his way up body until he finds my lips. Brushing his soft lips over mine, I taste myself as he gazes down at me through hooded, dark eyes. I take hold of his shoulders as I feel his erection thump lightly against me.

He lifts his body and, with his eyes still on me, he drives into me in one fluid motion. I whimper, every muscle clenching around him tightly.

I need to feel more.

Moving my legs, I wrap them around his waist, pulling him closer to me. Slowly, he withdraws, and instantly I miss what we share, before he drives back in forcefully, his eyes still fixed on me.

"Please, don't stop," I murmur, gripping onto him tighter.

I moan as he repeats what he's done. My mindless pleasure is building again, but I'm not ready for the fall. Not yet.

He's leisurely working in and out of me at a steady pace. I'm lost to the all-consuming pressure that is building from deep within. I've no control over it as the fire spreads. I grab his face in my hands and his mouth crushes against mine as he continues to drive in and out at an accelerated pace, rolling his hips against me.

I'm struggling to hold it together.

My grip on his face tightens; a silent signal that I'm at that point of no return. He groans and bites on my lips, pushing himself forward as far as he can go. With one more rotation of his hips, we both cry out.

I let go, feeling him throb and then tense deep inside me.

Our deep and desperate kiss changes pace as our bodies relax. I might not understand all my feelings, but in this moment, I'm certain my feelings for Connor Andrews have changed yet again to something deeper than I thought possible. And as I kiss him slowly, I'm sure he knows the words I won't yet bring myself to say.

He pulls back and the smile on his face is almost ridiculous as he watches me, and then he frowns. Yes, he knows the meaning behind my kiss. "What's wrong?" I ask softly, my voice full of concern.

"Nothing, except I'm happy." He pulls his body away from me

reluctantly. "I also seem to have worked up an appetite."

"I'm not surprised. Why don't we go and have a relaxing bath and, if you're good, I'll cook."

"That sounds like the best offer a man can get, although I wouldn't hold much hope on getting a relaxing bath, because I already want you all over again."

"Well, then I'm all yours for the taking."

Chapter 30

I'M SICK.

No, I feel as though I'm dying. Julie's had the cold. Even Connor had a head cold over the weekend, and what do I get? Full on man flu, and I can really do without it. Aches and pains course through my body. What a way to start a new week. All I want to do is crawl into bed in a darkened room and sleep, but I can't; I'm halfway through reading this new script Trevor has sent me.

Trevor is desperately waiting for my thoughts on this, and so far, so good. He's excited about this one; he and my dad can't stop talking about it. *The Turning Point*. It's a romance about a young woman who has come to a crossroads in her life. She's not sure what she should do for the best moving forward. She's had a tough life, lived on the streets, been involved in all sorts, but ultimately, she wants something better. A better life for herself. A job. She's not looking for much, just the basics.

It's a great storyline. Maybe it's because I've been there at the crossroads. Been unsure of what happens next, what path to follow. I really am getting sucked straight into the story and, when reading a script, that can make or break it for me.

"Ella, Julie is coming over. She'll stay with you while I'm out."

"Connor, I don't need looking after. I have the flu, that's all. Now go and look at apartments. I wish I was fit enough to make sure they're all decent inside." I have no idea what I'll do when he moves out into his own place, but he's right, he has to do it for himself. And I can't expect him to stay here with me when another man has shared my home. It's still early days in our relationship, so maybe this will work out well for us. We can do the whole dating thing, as opposed to living together.

"Just humour me, will you? Anyway, Julie wanted to see you. There's soup in the fridge; Callum brought it around earlier. If you need me to bring anything in, drop me a text. I shouldn't be too long."

"Okay. Go on and get out of here."

He bends down and kisses my nose. "See you later," he says before leaving me curled up on the couch watching TV. I hate daytime TV. I would hate to sit in the house day after day and have nothing to look forward to other than this drivel.

I was meant to be meeting up with Jess and Alex today to talk through some of our ideas. We want to raise awareness to women who are in domestic abuse situations that there are places for them to go. There are people who can help them. Jess and I discovered after doing some research that a small percentage of woman who have been victims find themselves living on the streets because they have no one to turn to. No one to help them through what is a very difficult and traumatic time. It makes me sad that in our day and age things like this are still happening.

Jess is passionate about helping women who find themselves in dire circumstances and I'm just as passionate about helping out the homeless, and I'm sure with Alex's help, we can raise some much needed awareness for two great causes.

If I close my eyes and get some sleep, I might be able to do some research later and then reschedule my meeting with Jess and Alex later in the week. I know how busy they are. Alex has Libby, the kids, and an empire to run, and Jess has Fletcher, and a new baby, and her business, although she has said she doesn't know which one causes her more trouble. I couldn't help but laugh when she said that.

"I guess you couldn't wait to jump into bed with my best friend," Donovan slurs, wiping his mouth with the back of his hand after taking a drink from the bottle of beer in his hand.

"Oh, come on! Don't you dare, especially after all these months of you being in L.A., staying in my house and having other women in my bed."

He takes a step toward me and I step back. I don't want him anywhere near me. He stinks of alcohol and he looks like shit.

"What's wrong, Ella? Take a good look. You did this to me. You put me out on the streets. You took my job from me."

"And you took nothing from me? Everything that has happened has all been your own doing. You walked away from me after telling me you loved me, knowing what I would be facing."

He starts walking and I realise I have nowhere to go. "But I knew Daddy would help you. The guys I dealt with weren't going to be so patient. I did what I did to protect you."

"What do you mean?" I yell.

"What I mean, my gorgeous Ella . . ."

"I'm not yours."

He shakes his head in frustration. "They were coming for you if I didn't pay them what I owed. I was protecting you. I couldn't let them harm you." I'm gobsmacked by his revelation. The back of my legs hit the couch and I sink down, taking in what he's just said. He was protecting me.

"Ella, babe, I love you. That hasn't changed."

"But I've changed."

"Yes, you have. You've gone from my fun-loving, gorgeous girl to a slut. What is it? Do you think sleeping with Connor will get you something that I couldn't give you? Sleeping your way to the top doesn't suit you."

"It's funny, I already thought I was at the top of my game. Can you leave?"

"I'm not going anywhere. You and I need to talk about us."

"Donovan, there is no us. There hasn't been for four months. Please, just go. I don't have the energy for this today."

"No." He pushes me until my back is touching the fabric of the couch. Donovan sits down and puts his arm around my shoulders; I flinch under his touch. The smell of alcohol is so much stronger now he's right beside me. It's turning my stomach.

He puts his other hand on my knee. I look at his hand and then at his face. Whatever he thinks is going to happen here, I won't let it.

I try to stand up but his grip on my shoulder tightens. His face closes in and . . .

In a blind panic, I open my eyes. My heart is racing and tears stream down my face. It wasn't real, just a dream, I tell myself over and over. I can't control my breathing. I try to take deep breaths but I can't. I just end up gasping for air.

Everything in the room is blurry. I close my eyes and take several deep breaths, calming myself down. I reopen them and everything is as it should be. A dream. A stupid dream. I've not had one of those for weeks.

I thought I was long past this stage, but obviously, I was wrong.

Picking up my phone, I look at the time. Twelve-forty-five, and Julie has texted

I'm running late. Something came up but I'll see you soon.

I should text her back and tell her not to bother coming over, but there's no point, she'll come over anyway. My grumbling stomach tells me I should eat, although I'm not sure I can face it, but I could do with some water. I push the cover aside and stand up and walk through into the kitchen, my body shivering with cold.

Connor has me smiling and he's not even home. Sitting on the work surface is a bottle of cough medicine, a packet of tissues, and some painkillers, along with a note and a bar of chocolate.

Just in case you fancy some chocolate. C xx

He thinks of everything. I grab a bottle of water from the fridge and take the painkillers followed by the cough medicine. Then I take the tissues and make my way back into my front room and get myself comfortable on the couch.

Flicking through the channels, I find there's nothing worth watching. I almost jump from my seat hearing the front door close. The intercom didn't buzz so it must be either my dad or Callum, or maybe both of them. It can't be Julie; she always buzzes to get in. I really should give her a key for days like today when I can't be bothered moving.

"If you don't want to catch the flu, I would turn around and go home," I call out with a laugh. It's only one set of footsteps I hear crossing the floor. Maybe it's Connor home earlier than he planned.

"After travelling all this way to come home to you?" My heart falters hearing his voice. I begin to shake. I stare at him with wide eyes in disbelief that he has the cheek and audacity to be standing in my home, in my living room with a case in his hands, as though it's the most natural thing in the world.

I stare into his deep blue eyes and my chest aches, panic already setting in. My heart is racing. He puts his case down and takes a step toward me.

To be continued

Books by
KAREN FRANCES

THE CAPTURED SERIES
Family Ties a Captured Series Novella
He's Captured my Heart Book 1
He's Captured my Trust Book 2
He's Captured my Soul Book 3
She's Captured my Love Book 4
Captured by Our Addiction Book 5

A BEAUTIFUL GAME SERIES
Playing the Field, A Beautiful Game Novella
Playing the Game Book 1
Playing to Win Book 2
Saving the Game

Moving On a standalone

SCRIPTED SERIES
Scripted Reality Book 1
Scripted Love Book 2 Coming soon

About the Author

KAREN FRANCES IS THE AUTHOR of ten romance novels and two novellas.

She currently lives just outside Glasgow, Scotland, with her husband, five children and two dogs, although she does dream of living somewhere warm and sunny. Her days are spent helping her husband run their busy family business. She spends some of her free time trying to keep fit and prepare healthy meals for her family, when their busy schedules allow them to sit down at meal times together. The rest of her free time she uses to plot and write and occasionally read.

Karen writes stories that are both believable and full of life. More often than not she loves sending her readers on an emotional journey alongside her characters.

For more information
www.karenfrancesauthor.co.uk

Acknowledgements

I ALWAYS STRUGGLE WHEN IT comes to this part because there are always so many people who help on all different levels. From my writing career to my personal life. Through good times and bad times.

Every day I count myself lucky to have an amazing family and incredible friends who support me. I also have the most amazing team that help me bring my stories to life.

To my dear husband Paul and my gorgeous kids- Yes, I know we all drive each other crazy but isn't that what families do? I love you all unconditionally.

My gorgeous friends, we might not see or speak to each other every day, but that's okay because we all know we are there for each other. I love you all.

Janet, you may or may not know this but you have kept me sane when life was getting out of hand. Yes, we've known each other for what seems like forever, but I can't imagine not seeing or hearing your craziness every single day. You are a crazy c??? And yes I probably say that word more than you now.

Laura, Maxine and Suzie—You all help me on a daily basis, not just promoting me and my books but you are also there when I need advice or just someone to talk to. Thank you all for all your support.

Leah and April- Thank you once again for your feedback on the very first draft of Scripted Reality. And April thank you for helping me finally come up with a title.

Karen, my editor and friend- I love working with you and I love our whole crazy process of editing.

Kari, Kari March Designs- You rock. That's all.

Christine, Type A Formatting—What can I say? I love what you do.

Margaret, thank you for giving *Scripted Reality* a final read through for me.

Krissy—The sea may separate us but I know you are always there. Love you lady.

Bloggers—I take my hat off to all the bloggers around the world. You are all amazing and do an incredible job of promoting authors.

My readers group- you are an amazing bunch of ladies.

To the authors in the support group—I don't know what to say about you. You support, encourage, and offer advice and even listen to the odd moan. Thank you.

I know I'm bound to have missed someone out and for that I'm sorry, but I'd like to say I feel incredible fortunate to have made so many friends within the author community over the last few years.

26574213R00141

Printed in Poland
by Amazon Fulfillment
Poland Sp. z o.o., Wrocław